PUFFIN

THE CIRCUS DOGS OF PRAGUE

RACHELLE DELANEY is the author of *The Metro Dogs of Moscow*, which was shortlisted for the 2014 Silver Birch Award. Her first novel, *The Ship of Lost Souls*, was a finalist for the Sheila A. Egoff Children's Literature Prize, the Chocolate Lily Book Award, and the Red Cedar Book Award. In 2010, she won the Canadian Authors Association/Bookland Press Emerging Writer Award. When not writing novels, Delaney connects kids and nature through the David Suzuki Foundation.

Also by Rachelle Delaney

The Metro Dogs of Moscow
The Hunt for the Panther
The Lost Souls of Island X
The Ship of Lost Souls

THE CIRCUS DOGS OF PRAGUE

Rachelle Delaney

PUFFIN

PUFFIN

an imprint of Penguin Canada Books Inc.,
a Penguin Random House Company

Published by the Penguin Group
Penguin Canada Books Inc., 320 Front Street West, Suite 1400,
Toronto, Ontario M5V 3B6, Canada

Penguin Group (USA) LLC, 375 Hudson Street, New York, New York 10014, U.S.A.
Penguin Books Ltd, 80 Strand, London WC2R 0RL, England
Penguin Ireland, 25 St Stephen's Green, Dublin 2, Ireland
(a division of Penguin Books Ltd)
Penguin Group (Australia), 707 Collins Street, Melbourne, Victoria 3008,
Australia (a division of Pearson Australia Group Pty Ltd)
Penguin Books India Pvt Ltd, 11 Community Centre, Panchsheel Park,
New Delhi – 110 017, India
Penguin Group (NZ), 67 Apollo Drive, Rosedale, Auckland 0632, New Zealand
(a division of Pearson New Zealand Ltd)
Penguin Books (South Africa) (Pty) Ltd, 24 Sturdee Avenue, Rosebank,
Johannesburg 2196, South Africa

Penguin Books Ltd, Registered Offices: 80 Strand, London WC2R 0RL, England

First published 2014

2 3 4 5 6 7 8 9 10   (WEB)

Manufactured in Canada.

LIBRARY AND ARCHIVES CANADA CATALOGUING IN PUBLICATION

Delaney, Rachelle, author
The circus dogs of Prague / Rachelle Delaney.

ISBN 978-0-14-318416-4 (pbk.)

I. Title.
PS8607.E48254C57 2014   jC813'.6   C2014-900413-3

eBook ISBN 978-0-14-319189-6

Visit the Penguin Canada website at **www.penguinrandomhouse.ca**

For Jana

Contents

1

Acrophobia

After seven years of travelling the world, JR knew the airplane safety talk so well he could have given it himself. That is, if he could speak Human so the other passengers could understand him. And if he had opposable thumbs to demonstrate how to buckle a seat belt.

Nonetheless, he always listened carefully, noting the location of the four emergency exits on board the aircraft. A good Jack Russell terrier was always prepared to stage a rescue. Especially when travelling with George.

From his carrier at his human's feet, he watched the toe of George's Italian leather shoe tap-tap-tap the floor. George did that whenever he was frightened. Like when he watched movies with clowns in them. JR sent him calming vibes, but it was no use. Thanks to his well-tuned Terrier Senses, he could smell George's fear as clearly as he could smell the mini pretzels the flight attendants would hand out at snack time.

How he loved those pretzels.

It was surprising, really. As an employee of the Canadian Embassy, George had travelled all over the world with JR at his side. They'd lived in five cities and taken more weekend trips than either could remember. George had racked up so many frequent flyer points that the airlines sent him cards on his birthday. And yet, he was still terrified of flying.

JR tuned back in to the flight attendant, who was now showing them how to put on their oxygen masks "in the slim chance of an emergency." George's toe-tapping was getting louder and faster.

"Please secure your own masks before helping others," the flight attendant advised them, and JR thought this sound advice. He hoped George was taking good note, though judging by the frenzied toe-tapping, he rather doubted it.

In the seat beside George, Nadya was flipping through the in-flight magazine while humming a tune. JR recognized it as the theme song from the reality TV show about the figure skaters, which they watched every Thursday night, all three of them curled up on the couch. Thursdays were JR's favourite days.

Thankfully, he didn't have to worry about Nadya. In the slim chance of an emergency, she would secure her own mask first, then help both him and George secure theirs. Good old Nadya. He sent her loving vibes as the safety talk ended and the plane lumbered onto the runway. Where would they be without her?

It was thanks to Nadya that they were finally going to escape Moscow for a week in Prague. Apparently she had a brother, Nikolai, who worked for a travelling Russian circus that was passing through town. JR couldn't wait. Not that he disliked Moscow—after five months, it was finally starting to feel like home, despite the crazy drivers and the constant haze of exhaust. He now knew all the best-smelling spots in their neighbourhood, and he'd made some great friends, including some local strays.

But the entire summer had been unbearably hot and stiflingly smoggy. Even their twice-daily walks to the dog park (or "walkies," as George called them) had long since lost their appeal. Some days, the smog upset George's weak stomach so much that he could barely manage one quick walkie.

"Prague is more temperate," Nadya had promised. "We'll spend our days relaxing in outdoor cafés and taking long walks in the woods near the castle."

For JR, that was the clincher. Woods almost always involved small, squeaky things to chase. And maybe, just maybe, George would let him off-leash.

But perhaps best of all, JR's three closest friends had come along for the trip. He had Nadya to thank for that, too, for she had invited Beatrix, Robert, and Pie—and their humans, of course. Nadya was generous like that.

Unfortunately, JR's friends were all too big to travel in the cabin of the plane. They were all down below, in the Hold.

"And we're off!" exclaimed John Cowley, the Australian Ambassador to Russia and a good friend of George's, as the plane's nose tilted skyward and its wheels rose off the runway. JR didn't need his well-tuned Terrier Senses to hear George's whimper. He sent his human more calming vibes, hoping the air would be smooth so he could soon sit up on George's lap. That always helped keep him calm. And right now, it was very important that he keep George calm. In fact, he'd go so far as to say that everyone's happiness depended on it.

Which meant that everyone's happiness depended on JR.

Fortunately, a good Jack Russell terrier could always find a way to keep everyone happy.

A chime soon sounded, telling the humans they could unbuckle their seat belts and move around. JR scratched at the door of his carrier, and George leaned over and pulled him out, his hands sweaty and trembling. JR sat down in his lap and nosed his chest to let him know that everything would be okay.

Especially if the mini pretzels arrived soon.

"You never told me you were afraid of heights," Nadya murmured to George. She had the middle seat between him and John, who was peering out the window at the world below.

JR glanced up at his human, wondering how he'd managed to keep that one secret. George hated heights so much that he could live only in ground-floor apartments.

"Afraid of heights? What makes you say that?" George loosened his grip on his armrests.

"Look!" John pointed out the window. "I can see the Kremlin!"

"No thanks!" George yelped, squeezing his eyes shut.

Nadya raised an eyebrow at JR, who would have shrugged if his shoulders allowed it.

George opened one eye. "Okay, so I'm afraid of heights," he said. "It's a real condition, though, not just a little fear. They call it acrophobia."

"I see." Nadya reached over to pet JR, and he tilted his head so she had easy access to the sweet spot behind his left ear. She scratched it for a few moments, then turned back to George. "So let me get this straight. You're afraid of heights—"

"I've got acrophobia," he corrected her.

JR sighed into George's shirt.

"You've got acrophobia," Nadya repeated. "And you're also afraid of deep water."

George nodded. "That's called aquaphobia."

"Right." Nadya bit her lip. "Anything else?"

"Arachnophobia," George said before JR could get him to stop talking. "Fear of spiders."

JR couldn't tell what Nadya was thinking, but he was fairly certain she wasn't banking on George to save them in the slim chance of an emergency. He lay down on his side so she could rub his belly, and she smiled, obliging. George stroked his head, and JR sensed them both relax. It was a good thing he was there, and not down in the Hold.

For a moment, his belly filled with guilt as a picture of his friends popped to mind: all three of them curled up in their crates, surrounded by thundering engines. Fortunately, Robert and Beatrix had strong stomachs, which they'd assured him would stand the two-and-a-half-hour flight. And Pie had swallowed some sedatives that John had wrapped in cheese, so hopefully he was sleeping like a puppy.

JR sent them all some calming vibes as well, then turned his attention back to his humans.

"Yipes!" George squeaked as the plane dipped its wing slightly, making a slow turn. "Maybe this was a bad idea." He wrapped his big hands around JR's belly. "Maybe we should have stayed in Moscow."

"Nonsense." Nadya pried one of his hands off JR's rib cage and held it in hers. "I promise this will be worth it. You'll love Praha. That's what the locals call Prague," she added.

"I hear it's a beautiful city," John remarked, pulling out his guidebook. "A city for lovers, that's what they say."

Nadya nodded, eyes shining. "It's one of the most beautiful cities in Europe. And my brother found us a rental apartment right in the centre of town, close to the river and the castle." She gave George's hand another squeeze. "I can't wait for you to meet Nikolai. And his daughter, Masha, too."

George managed a weak smile and smooshed JR's ears with a big, sweaty hand. JR grimaced and tried hard not to nip him.

Was there a "phobia" word for fear of commitment? he wondered. He made a mental note to ask Beatrix when they landed in Prague. If anyone would know, it was her.

Whatever it was called, George had a bad case of it—perhaps even worse than his fear of heights. JR couldn't remember him ever actually agreeing to meet a girlfriend's family. This would be a big step for him.

He spread himself out on George's lap so he couldn't go anywhere, not even to the tiny washroom at the back of the plane. There was always a chance he might decide not to come back out.

Paws-down, Nadya was the best thing that had happened to him and George in a long time. Maybe even ever. She was kind and smart and endlessly patient with George's ways. She even referred to them as his "quirks," even though everyone knew that "quirks" was just a polite way of saying "annoying habits."

Also, Nadya was always up for walkies. And she was never late for dinner, arriving with a dog treat tucked in her pocket, then humming while she helped George prepare the food (or rather, fixed whatever he was trying to make).

She made their little grey apartment feel like home.

"Is Nikolai older or younger than you?" John asked Nadya.

"Niko is my big brother," Nadya answered. "Growing up, he was my idol. I'd follow him around everywhere, and he always let me. He was so good-natured, so full of joy." She paused, and her smile faded a bit. "These days, though, he's different," she said. "Ever since he and his wife split up, about

five years ago, he's been … quieter. Sullen, sometimes. Except when he's flying. Then he's … How
do you say?" She tapped her chin, trying to find the
right words. "He's in his happy place."

"Your brother *likes* to fly?" George looked
incredulous.

Nadya laughed. "You have to if you're a trapeze artist."

"A circus trapeze artist." John whistled. "Now
that's an interesting career. Your parents couldn't
have been thrilled when Niko ran away to join
the circus."

Nadya shook her head. "It wasn't like that at
all. You see, the circus is a huge part of Russian
life. When I was growing up, people gave circus
performers the same respect as great scientists,
even astronauts."

"Really?" asked John. "How fascinating."

Nadya nodded. "And Niko is the star of
his show. Everyone loves the man on the flying
trapeze."

"Hey, is Niko with the company we saw?"
George asked, brightening. "Circus Magnificus?"

JR groaned inwardly. He knew all about Circus
Magnificus. George, Nadya, and John had gone to
a performance earlier in the summer, and George
had talked of little else for days after. Circus
Magnificus was world renowned for its daring

stunts and flashy costumes. Tickets weren't cheap, but apparently it had been worth it. George had returned home so inspired that he'd gone straight to the kitchen, grabbed three dessert plates, and proceeded to juggle them. JR had hightailed it to the bedroom and stayed under the bed until the mess had been cleaned up.

Nadya shook her head. "Niko performs with a small, traditional troupe called Circus Sergei. Actually," she said after a moment's pause, "I'd rather you didn't tell him we saw Circus Magnificus."

"Why's that?" John asked.

"Circus Magnificus has made Niko's life … difficult lately," she began. "You see—"

Just then, the plane flew through an air pocket and bounced. Just once. Just a small bounce.

Just enough to send George into a tizzy.

He yelped and gripped JR with both hands, driving his big thumbs into JR's ribs. JR let out a howl.

Every passenger on board turned to stare at them.

"Is everything all right, sir?" A flight attendant appeared at George's shoulder.

"Yes!" George gasped. "Yes, we're fine!" He smooshed JR's ears again.

The flight attendant looked from George to JR and back. "Maybe your dog needs to go back in his carrier," she said.

JR gasped. *Him?* She was blaming *him?*

"JR is fine," Nadya said quickly.

"Yeah," George added. "He's just ... afraid of heights. It's called acrophobia, you know."

JR almost bit his sweaty hand.

"Are you sure?" The flight attendant didn't look convinced.

"Oh yeah." George nodded. "It's a real condition, you know."

Sometimes, JR didn't know why he tried.

"Actually," Nadya said, "he could use a snack. Do you have any mini pretzels?"

If JR hadn't been anchoring George to his seat, he would have abandoned his human's lap for Nadya's.

He sent her more loving vibes as he watched her pry George's fingernails out of the holes they'd made in his armrest.

Nadya was the reason why he tried.

2
Terrier Senses

"Philophobia," Beatrix informed JR when he asked her. "That's the fear of love. I bet that's what your human suffers from." She tossed her big head of black-and-grey hair. Beside her, John Cowley sputtered as he received a mouthful of it.

"What do you call the fear of being stuck in a tiny car with too many dogs?" Robert asked, trying to turn in a circle but failing. "'Cause I've got it. Big time."

John and the dogs—JR, Beatrix, and the Australian shepherds, Robert and Pie—were crammed in the back seat of a little hatchback. It had been the only rental car left at the airport when they'd arrived, so they'd had to make do.

Up front, Nadya was driving, and George sat beside her, studying the streets of Prague on the tiny map on his phone. Nadya had given him the job of directing them to their neighbourhood, which was called Josefov. JR was keeping a close eye on them, counting down the minutes till George's weak stomach rebelled against reading in the car. He was already starting to look a little green.

"Or the fear of getting sick in that car?" Pie yawned, still sleepy from the sedatives.

Beatrix turned to him. "Are you going to be sick?"

Pie considered this for a moment, then nodded thoughtfully. "It's possible."

"Ugh." She tossed her hair again.

John flinched as it swatted him in the face. "Whose idea was it to bring the fluffy one?" he muttered, inching farther away from her.

"Fluffy?" Beatrix shot him a glare. "Pomeranians are fluffy. We keeshonds are *voluminous.*"

Pie whined. Robert grumbled. JR tried his best to tune them all out and focus on George and Nadya.

It had actually been Nadya's idea to bring the fluffy—or voluminous—one. She'd originally invited both Beatrix and her human, Johanna Van Wingerden. But Johanna, who worked for the Dutch Embassy, wasn't able to take time off.

They would have simply gone on without her had Beatrix not suddenly collapsed at the dog park the previous day. Convinced her prized purebred was suffering from extreme heat exhaustion,

Johanna had begged Nadya to take Beatrix with them to temperate Prague.

Nadya had crouched down to stroke Beatrix's fur, and Beatrix uttered a pathetic whimper. "Of course we'll take her," Nadya declared.

"Really?" George looked dubious. "But she's so ... big."

"It's all hair," Johanna assured him. "Underneath, she's actually quite petite."

"It's no problem," Nadya said, standing up. "Maybe it's because I was never allowed to have pets growing up, but I truly believe you can't have too many. The more the merrier, as they say."

At that, Beatrix had opened her eyes just long enough to wink at JR. Beatrix was not one to get left behind. JR had learned this months ago, when he'd first started sneaking out at night to explore Moscow with his new stray friends. As soon as Beatrix found out, she'd insisted on coming—and inviting an international contingent of embassy dogs along. It had taken JR a while to get used to them all.

Still, as happy as he was to be travelling with his friends, JR wasn't so sure about Nadya's "the more the merrier" theory. He and George, for instance, had no room in their lives for another dog. Just the thought of it—having to share his treats and walkies and couch time—made him shudder.

"How long do you think it'll be before we get there?" Pie asked in a small voice.

"You gonna lose your lunch?" Robert asked him.

"No," said Pie. "But I might lose the banana peel I ate in the parking lot."

JR sent Nadya some hurry-up vibes. Outside the window, old cream-coloured buildings with red rooftops whizzed by, shaded by big, leafy trees. Every now and then, he caught a glimpse of a great, shining river in the distance.

"I can't wait to explore this place!" Robert pranced. "I want outta this car!"

"You're stepping on my paw!" Beatrix snapped.

"I probably shouldn't have eaten that candy wrapper either." Pie sighed.

"Aw, your paw's fine."

"Well, my hair isn't. Would you move over?"

"Yes, I am definitely going to be sick."

Just as JR was ready to yell at them all to *shut up and let him focus*, Nadya turned a sharp right and threw the car into park in front of a small, red apartment building with white trim.

"We're here!" she announced.

They burst outside the moment John opened the back door—Robert leaping and twisting in the air, Beatrix tossing her head every which way, Pie dry-heaving on the cobblestones.

JR took in big gulps of air. In the summer, their neighbourhood in Moscow smelled like the exhaust of a thousand cars and the sweat of a million humans. Josefov smelled a bit like that, too, but it held other scents as well. Like dirt and dry grass and poplar leaves.

JR sucked it all in.

"Nice place your brother found us," John commented, looking up at the apartment building. "Will he be staying here, too?"

Nadya shook her head. "He and Masha stay on the circus grounds, in their little caravan. We'll go find them after we settle in."

"Psst," Robert hissed in JR's ear. "Now's our chance."

JR looked away from George. "Chance for what?"

Robert gave him an exasperated look. "We're off-leash! Let's get outta here while we can!"

JR hesitated, looking back at George. Though the colour was returning to his face, it still wasn't the best time to leave him alone. On the other paw, JR *was* off-leash. And if his Terrier Senses were right (which they always were), there were cats nearby. It had been ages since he'd had a good cat chase.

"Robert, no!" Pie protested, but it was too late. Robert was off and running around the side of the apartment building. Beatrix was right behind him, and JR wouldn't have been a very good terrier if he hadn't let his legs follow before his brain could decide whether it was really a good idea.

John and George hollered after them, but they ran on, heading for the back of the building, where they found a nice shady courtyard surrounded by similar red apartment buildings.

And there, in the middle of it, were three cats. One was a tabby, another was black with white splotches, and the third was a fluffy, long-haired grey. They lolled in the grass, cleaning their paws and swapping gossip like they hadn't a care in the world.

"Felines!" Beatrix cried.

"Let's get 'em!" JR yelled.

"Attack!" Robert hollered, dashing out in front. "Take no prisoners!"

The cats looked up in alarm.

"Dogs!" screeched the long-haired grey.

"Run!" yowled the black and white.

They scattered.

"Dibs on the tabby!" Beatrix called, digging her claws into the grass and taking a sharp right as her target headed for a shrub. Robert chased the black-and-white cat across the courtyard, hooting like a cowboy.

That left JR with the long-haired grey. He gave chase, tearing after her as she zigged and zagged, leaping over flower beds and dodging small trees.

JR stayed focused and low to the ground. There was nothing in the world like a good cat chase. It felt divine.

But just as he was closing the gap between them, the cat switched tactics, hanging a left and leaping up into the air. She landed halfway up the trunk of a tree, dug in her claws, and scampered up into the branches.

JR was already in the air by the time he realized where she was headed. He didn't have the option of gripping the trunk, and could only crash into it with a resounding *thunk*. He slid to the ground and scrambled to his feet, hoping no one had witnessed the collision.

"Gotcha!" he yelled up at the cat, as if he'd meant to tree her all along. He added a few more barks for good measure, daring her to come down.

High above him, the furball settled on a branch and looked down at him coolly. Then she resumed cleaning her paws.

Elsewhere in the courtyard, Robert and Beatrix were yapping as well, which made JR feel better. At least his wasn't the only cat that got away.

"Nice try, bonehead!" the tabby taunted from high up on the fence separating their courtyard from the next.

"Come down and say that to my face, hairball!" Beatrix retorted. "See what happens!"

JR turned back to his own cat and barked some more, just because he could. Just because he felt terrific. Better than he'd felt in—

"JR!"

He froze in mid-bark. Not because the voice was loud and sharp and disapproving.

Because it was Nadya's.

"JR, stop that *right now!*"

JR turned in disbelief. He'd never heard Nadya raise her voice at anyone before—not even George when he'd tried to juggle the dessert plates. It had never even occurred to him that she *could* yell.

His tail drooped between his legs.

"Get away from that cat!" Nadya commanded, marching over. "George, stop him!"

"Now, now." George pranced on the grass behind her, trying not to dirty his Italian leather shoes. "He's just playing. You wouldn't have hurt the kitty, right, JR?"

JR blinked innocently, glad for once that he couldn't speak Human and therefore didn't have to lie.

"He can't help it," George went on. "He's a terrier. This is what they do."

JR abandoned his tree and went to sit on George's wet feet. Despite his weak stomach and fear of practically everything, George wasn't so bad.

Nadya stopped and sighed. "You're right. I'm sorry, JR." She leaned over and held out her hand. JR hesitated for a moment, for she *had* treated him unfairly. But he was a forgiving dog, so he let her pet him. "You wouldn't hurt a cat, would you? I'm sorry for doubting you."

JR turned his head so she could scratch his ear. Humans could be so dense.

Then Nadya straightened, dug into her pocket, and pulled out a dog biscuit.

JR wagged his tail. Good old Nadya. She knew how to apologize. He sat down in the grass and waited for his gift.

But she turned away and stepped toward the tree.

As JR watched, open-mouthed, she proceeded to offer the biscuit—his biscuit—to the fluffy, long-haired grey, who was studying her from the branches.

"Come on, kitty," Nadya said in a high, squeaky voice JR had never heard her use. "I know it's a dog treat, but you'll like it anyway. Come out and get it."

"What's she doing?" Beatrix appeared beside JR.

"I-I-I don't know," he whispered.

"Maybe she's luring it out so we can chase it again?" Robert suggested, joining them.

"I think she's ..." JR swallowed hard, not wanting to say it. "*Feeding* it."

Beatrix and Robert gasped.

JR tore his eyes away from Nadya and looked to George to do something. But George was intent on rubbing a grass stain off his shoe.

John and Pie jogged around the corner.

"Sorry we took so long," Pie said breathlessly. "I just couldn't hold it, so we had to—" He stopped, taking in the scene. "Is that a *cat*?"

"No, Pie, it's a monkey," Robert answered.

"Huh." Pie cocked his head to the side. "Doesn't look like any monkey I've ever seen. But I suppose I've never met a Czech monkey," he added.

Robert sighed.

Pie went to investigate, returning a few moments later. "Yes," he reported. "I'm pretty sure that's a cat. A cute, fluffy one, too."

Beatrix looked horrified. "Cute?" she cried. "Cats aren't cute! Cats are horrible, hairy, shifty-eyed beasts!"

"Oh." Pie shrank back. "I ... I must not have looked closely enough."

"They're selfish, too," added Robert. "And lazy." He shook his head at Nadya. "She doesn't actually like cats, does she?"

"No way," JR said quickly. "She ... she must just be overtired."

"Plane rides are tiring," Pie agreed, yawning. "I bet she just needs a good nap."

"Right." JR nodded hard. "Yeah, that must be it."

"It's probably a stray." John frowned up at the cat. "Best stay away from it."

"But she's so pretty," Nadya cooed.

"Ew." Beatrix grimaced. "Did a suitcase fall on her head?"

"She reminds me of my neighbour's cat, growing up," Nadya went on. "Niko and I would care for her when her owners went on holiday. She was so lovely." The cat smoothed her whiskers, clearly flattered.

Now JR had had enough. He took hold of George's trouser leg and tugged hard.

George looked down. "Hungry, boy?" He checked his watch. "I guess it is almost dinnertime. We should go inside and unpack." He turned and headed back around front. John, the shepherds, and Beatrix fell in line behind him.

Nadya lingered a moment, still looking up at the cat, then turned and followed the others. JR took up the rear, herding them all back in. He didn't even pause to look back at the beast in the tree.

If he never saw her again, it would be too soon.

3
Circus Family

Their Josefov apartment turned out to be centuries old, with lots of dusty crannies to explore. The wooden floors were nice and creaky and the walls overrun by squeaky things. It was only a matter of time before one emerged for a good chase.

Unfortunately, the dogs had barely begun to explore when it was time to go again—this time to meet Nadya's brother and niece.

"It's not far," Nadya promised as they piled back into the car. "The circus always sets up at Letna Park, just across the river and up the hill. Maybe we'll walk up there tomorrow."

"Hope we get to go, too," Robert said as he squeezed into the back seat. "I never thought I'd be sick of car rides, but I'd definitely pass on another."

Fortunately, Nadya was right. Less than ten minutes later, they tumbled back out to find themselves in a big, grassy park criss-crossed with walking paths.

"This is very civilized." Beatrix nodded her approval.

"Where's the circus?" George shaded his eyes from the sun and squinted around. "I expected a big top."

"There will be," Nadya promised. "It only just arrived—Opening Day is still four days away. But the circus springs up almost overnight. You'll see when we return tomorrow—it's like magic."

She then led them across the park to a concrete platform where they could look out on the entire city: a sea of red roofs with islands of leafy trees, ringed by a great, shining river.

"That's the Vltava." Nadya pointed at the river. "It runs from the north of the country all the way to the south." She sighed. "Isn't Prague lovely?"

"No wonder my guidebook also calls it a city for artists," said John. "There's inspiration in the air."

"I don't know about inspiration." Robert sniffed. "But there's definitely dumplings."

"John's right," said Pie. "I've felt inspired ever since I got here. In fact, I'm working on a new poem."

Robert winked at JR, who hid a chuckle. Pie had recently discovered his love of the performing arts when their search for some missing strays in

Moscow had landed them all onstage at a fashion show. He'd been holding regular spoken word performances at the dog park ever since.

"Nadya!" someone called. "Tetya Nadya!"

They all turned to see a young girl sprinting across the grass. About ten years old, she had a big smile and long, brown braids that were quickly unravelling.

"Masha!" Nadya cried, running to meet her. She swept the girl up in a hug, and the two launched into some merry Russian chatter.

Pie and Beatrix hung back, but Robert trotted over to give the girl a good sniff, and JR followed, fairly certain she had gingerbread cookies in her pockets. As usual, his nose was correct. Hopefully she'd share.

"This is my niece, Masha." Nadya turned the girl around by her shoulders so everyone could see her. She had a round face like Nadya's and freckles on her nose and cheeks. "She's so much bigger than the last time I saw her." Nadya hugged Masha again. "She speaks good English, too, don't you, Masha?"

Masha nodded. "Welcome to Prague!" she said proudly, and George and John stepped up to shake her hand.

"Where is your father, dear?" Nadya asked.

Masha looked up in surprise. "You didn't see him?"

Nadya shook her head, and Masha pointed at a flagpole some twenty feet away.

"Where?" Nadya squinted. Then she gasped.

JR craned his neck for a better view, but all he could see was a tall pole, maybe twenty feet tall, with a big flag near the top.

Except, he realized as he stared longer, it wasn't a flag at all.

It was a man.

"What the—" JR did a double take. "Guys, look! There's a man on that pole!"

George yelped.

"What's he doing up there?" Pie cried.

"Is he okay?" John asked. "Should we get help?"

Nadya shushed them. "He's fine," she whispered. "He's my brother, Niko, and he's practising."

"It's his Chinese Pole routine," Masha added, crouching down beside the dogs to watch.

The pole had no handholds, nothing to help Niko stay balanced horizontally like a human flag. As they watched, he turned and lowered his legs until his feet found the pole. Then he proceeded to climb even higher, right to the very top.

"This is my favourite part," Masha whispered, putting an arm around Pie.

Slowly, carefully, Niko flipped himself upside down, until his feet were at the top of the pole and his head about six feet below. Then he let go of the pole, so he was hanging only by his feet.

"This is incredible," John breathed.

"This is t-t-terrifying!" George covered his eyes, peeking through his fingers.

"Now!" said Masha.

As if on command, Niko let go of the pole with his feet and began to plummet straight for the earth.

"No!" George shrieked.

"I can't watch!" Pie buried his head in Masha's shoulder.

But before JR could even shut his eyes, Niko stopped, a mere two inches above the ground.

He had stopped his fall using only his feet.

For a moment, no one said a word. Then John punched the air. "Bravo!" he cried. Nadya whistled.

Masha hugged Pie. "Isn't he amazing?"

Niko flipped over, stood up, and dusted off his pants. He began to stroll their way as if he'd done nothing out of the ordinary.

"Well." Robert grinned. "I think it's safe to say our boy Niko does not suffer from acrophobia."

Dinner that night involved a hearty Czech goulash, cooked on a tiny stove in Niko and Masha's caravan. Their entire home was little more than a single room with two beds, a table, sink, and stove.

While the humans chatted and slurped their goulash, Masha made sure the dogs didn't miss out, slipping them bits of dumplings under the table. After dinner, she joined them on the floor, and JR laid his head in her lap, sending her thankful vibes. Masha was a good human—he could sense that as clearly as he could sense her father's discontent.

Exactly what was wrong with Niko, JR had yet to determine. But the man certainly was twitchy, and had been ever since he'd hopped off the flagpole.

Nadya seemed to sense it, too. "I can't wait to see you perform again," she told Niko as she topped up his wineglass. "It's been years, hasn't it?"

Good old Nadya. She would have made a decent Jack Russell terrier herself. JR sent her affectionate vibes.

"I'm getting excited about Opening Day," said John.

But Nadya shook her head. "We'll go on the second day," she told him. "Niko doesn't let family or friends watch on Opening Day."

"Why not?" asked George.

"The second show is always better," Niko said simply.

"Also, he thinks it's bad luck," Nadya added, poking her brother in the ribs. "He's superstitious."

Niko shrugged. "Lots of circus performers are," he said. "I know acrobats who refuse to wear green in the big top because they think it's bad luck. Same with whistling in the dressing room."

"Really?" John chuckled. "How strange."

"I understand completely," Pie told the dogs. "I always eat exactly seven squares of toilet paper the morning of a big performance."

"Yeah, but you do that every day," said Robert.

Pie shook his head. "Usually, it's three."

"My mother won't perform without a clove of garlic sewn into her leotard," Masha piped up.

"Is your mother a performer, too?" George asked, not catching the tight-lipped look Nadya was giving him, an obvious signal to change the subject.

Masha nodded. "She's a tightrope walker."

Fortunately, before Nadya had to change the topic herself, there was a knock on the door. And before anyone could rise to answer it, the door opened and a stout, grey-haired man poked his head inside.

"Sergei!" Niko was on his feet in a moment.

"Sergei?" Pie gasped, leaping up, too. "As in *Circus* Sergei?"

The man glanced around at all the humans and dogs squished inside the caravan, and said something in Russian.

"Family," Niko explained, in English. "This is my sister Nadya, her friends George and John, and their dogs. Everyone, this is Sergei, our director."

Nadya rose to shake the man's hand. "So nice to meet you," she said. "We're big fans of your circus."

"Well then." Sergei smoothed his rumpled blazer. "Welcome." He spoke English well, but with a heavy accent. "Niko, I came to talk about your pole routine. I saw you practising today."

"Oh." Niko straightened. "I didn't see you there."

Sergei nodded. "It's a very good routine."

"Isn't it brilliant?" said Nadya.

Niko frowned at her. "Thank you," he told Sergei.

There was a pause, and JR could sense Niko holding his breath.

"But I want you to stick to the trapeze," Sergei finished. "You're the star of the show—everyone comes to see the man on the flying trapeze."

"Oh but—" Nadya began to protest, then stopped when her brother shot her another look.

"Right." Niko nodded at his feet.

"Yes," Sergei said. "You'll stick to the trapeze." He turned to go, and his gaze fell on the dogs and Masha. "Again with the animals, Masha?" He shook his head, then turned back to Niko. "I found her in the barn today."

Niko turned his frown on his daughter. "Masha, we spoke about this."

"But the elephant was limping!" she protested. "I had to check on him."

"The barn is no place for a young lady," Sergei told her. "You should focus on getting to dance class on time."

With that, he nodded goodbye to the humans and left.

Niko and Masha sighed in unison.

"What was that about?" Nadya demanded. "What does he mean, you can't do your new routine? It's amazing!"

Niko sank back down in his chair. "Sergei," he said, picking up his wineglass, "hates change. Unfortunately, there's nothing this circus needs more right now."

Masha sighed again, and JR laid his head back down in her lap.

"Years ago, we had no problem selling out a show," Niko continued. "These days, we perform for rows of empty seats. Now everyone goes to see Circus Magnificus instead."

"Circus Magnificus!" George exclaimed. "We saw—"

Recalling Nadya's request back on the plane, JR barked sharply, cutting George off just in time.

"—a poster about it." George gulped.

"An ugly one at that," John added. "Looked boring, didn't it?" he asked George.

"You'd never catch me paying $64.95 for a ticket," George declared.

"Circus Magnificus," Niko snapped, "is all flash and shine and money. *Big* money. The small traditional circus, though, has heart." He drained his wineglass and set it down with a *thump*.

Another uncomfortable pause ensued. Pie began to maul his toenail.

Finally, Nadya cleared her throat. "You'll never guess what I saw today," she told her brother brightly. "A cat just like the one our neighbours had when we were small. Do you remember? What was her name?"

JR grimaced. Of all the topics Nadya could have chosen, she had to pick the cat.

Niko shook his head, looking uninterested. "A stray?" he asked. Nadya nodded. "Prague is full of stray cats. Hundreds of thousands of them." He wrinkled his nose.

JR was liking Niko more and more. He sent the man some affectionate vibes, then flipped onto his back so Masha could rub his belly. They were both good humans. Good humans in need of some cheering up.

Perhaps by the end of the week, he could find a way to make them happy, too.

4

Kisa

The next morning, JR awoke in a nice, warm sunbeam. He yawned, stretched, and began to prepare his Terrier Senses for the day ahead by identifying all the smells around him. There was the scent of charred wood from the fireplace beside his bed. And the scent of last night's goulash, which still clung to the jackets in the closet.

And something else, too. JR breathed in again, trying to place it. It was something ...

Something ...

Hairy.

He shot up in bed and looked around. On his right lay Beatrix, snoring softly. On his left lay the shepherds, herding sheep in their sleep. But it wasn't any of them he smelled. It was a different animal altogether.

A squeaky thing, maybe? He took another deep breath.

No.

It was a cat.

He was on his feet in a second, spinning in a tight circle, trying to find it.

"Would you stop?" Beatrix moaned.

"There's a cat! In the house!" JR yelped, spinning in the opposite direction.

"What?" His friends all leaped to their feet, shaking off sleep.

"Are you sure?" gasped Pie.

"I smell it!" Robert yelled. "Cat in the house!"

"Intruder!" Beatrix bellowed. "Find the cat!"

They scattered, yapping and yelping. Robert took the living room, while Beatrix beelined for the kitchen. Pie scampered off to John's room, and JR headed for George and Nadya's. The door was open, so he zipped inside, only to be hit full-on by the sour, musky, disgusting smell of *cat*.

He didn't even realize he was barking his head off until George shouted, "JR! Be quiet!"

He stopped to catch his breath.

George was sitting up in bed, wearing his pyjamas with the sailboat print. His hair was a mess, but not the orderly kind of mess he spent half an hour each day trying to achieve. A truly messy mess.

"You want to what?" George asked Nadya, looking very confused.

JR looked from his human to his human's girl-friend, and nearly fainted dead away.

There, in Nadya's arms, was a cat.

But not just any cat. The fluffy grey cat he'd treed the day before.

His Terrier Senses kicked in again, and he began barking uncontrollably.

"JR!" George yelled again. "Be quiet!"

"Yes, JR. Hush," added Nadya. Then she turned back to George. "I said, I want to adopt her."

The cat's eyes lit up.

JR's jaw dropped.

"What'd she say?" Robert poked his snout over JR's shoulder.

"She better not have said what I think she said." Beatrix pushed them both aside so she could get a good look at the scene. "Ugh! I don't believe this!"

JR tried to repeat Nadya's words, but his mouth had gone completely dry. This had to be a dream. Yes. He was still in bed, asleep, and this was last night's dumplings talking. He should never have eaten five.

"What's going on?" John appeared behind them, peeking into the bedroom. He did a double take. "That's a cat!"

"Thanks, Ambassador Obvious," Beatrix growled. "What is *wrong* with these people?"

"Is that the cat from yesterday?" asked John.

Nadya nodded, stroking the cat's head.

"Whoa," Robert breathed.

"Adopt her?" John repeated, rubbing the morning stubble on his chin. "Are you sure?"

"No," George answered, just as Nadya said, "Yes."

"I'm confused," Pie said, chewing on his tail.

"This is just absurd." Beatrix stamped her paw. "Why would they want a cat?"

"Reckon you could mop the floor with that one," Robert mused.

"I th-think …" JR stuttered. "Sh-she wants it for … a pet."

"A pet!" Pie dropped his tail and wiggled like a puppy. "What fun! She'll be like a new little sister! We can take her for walks and play games and—"

He stopped under the stony glares of his friends. "Or not." He turned back to his tail.

John frowned. "She's a stray, Nadya. She might be dirty."

"I'll wash her," Nadya replied, scratching the cat's head. "Yes, she's just like the cat I loved growing up. I wanted a pet so badly, but my parents always refused."

The cat began to purr. She sounded like the dishwasher George and JR had in their apartment in Dublin.

How he'd hated that dishwasher.

George tugged on his messy hair. "You know, they might not let her in when we get back to Moscow," he pointed out.

"Why not?" Nadya asked. "They let JR in."

"She did *not* just say that," Beatrix gasped.

"Ouch," said Robert.

JR flinched like he'd been kicked in the stomach.

"I'll look into it," Nadya went on. "I'm sure there's a way to get her home with us."

"Well then." John sighed. "I guess the cat stays for now. And I for one am in need of some coffee." He headed for the kitchen to make it.

"I'm going to bathe Kisa," said Nadya.

"Kisa?" George repeated.

"It's Russian for 'kitty.'" Nadya smiled.

And she turned and walked past the dogs, the cat still cradled in her arms.

JR followed his friends back to the living room, feeling like he had the time George took him to get a canine root canal. Completely numb, from nose to tail.

"Are you okay, JR?" Pie whispered, sidling up close.

JR resisted the urge to yell, "My humans are adopting a cat! Do you *think* I'm okay?" Somehow, he forced himself to nod.

"Well, I'm not," Beatrix said. "I don't want to share my space with any cat, let alone a *stray.*" She smoothed her whiskers. "We're all going to get fleas, I just know it. If I come home with fleas, Johanna is going to lose her mind."

"Strays aren't so bad," Pie protested. "You said so yourself after we got to know the street dogs in Moscow."

"That's different," Beatrix said quickly. "The Moscow strays are smart, and surprisingly tidy. But most important, they're dogs."

"Bea's right, Pie," said Robert. "Cats are a whole different ball of fur. They're shifty little things."

"Devious," added Beatrix.

"I wouldn't trust 'em as far as I could throw 'em," said Robert. "Which was about three feet, last time I tried."

JR headed for his bed, where he sat down and shut his eyes. What would the Moscow strays do in his position? he wondered. He pictured Ania, the cool pack leader, and wise old Boris who rarely left her side. Neither of them would let a human introduce a cat into their family—that was for sure. But then, Boris and Ania didn't have to rely on humans for food and walkies.

"Once I'm finished cleaning and feeding Kisa, we can go exploring," Nadya called from the bathroom. "I'll show you a few sights on our way back up to the circus grounds."

"All right," John replied from the kitchen. "I want to see the Charles Bridge before it gets too busy. And let's take the dogs with us. My guidebook says Prague is very dog-friendly."

"We get to go exploring!" Pie turned to JR. "That's exciting, isn't it? You love exploring."

JR had no answer for that. He laid his head on his paws, wishing they were all back in Moscow. That they'd never left in the first place.

"Oh, come on." Pie nosed him in the ribs. "Everything's going to be okay. I bet you'll like having a new little sister."

JR began to count backward from ten.

"Maybe Pie's right," Robert agreed.

"What?" JR sat up and whirled to face him.

"You can't be serious," Beatrix snapped.

"I am," said Robert. "Think about it. We can chase that floor mop whenever we want! We'll ambush her when she least expects it! Ha ha!" He pounced on an imaginary cat, then did a little victory dance.

"Robert, no!" Pie protested.

"Well, that's true," Beatrix admitted. "But I'd rather not have the fleaball around at all."

JR sank back down and closed his eyes. Over the sound of running water in the bathroom, Nadya was humming the theme song from the reality show about the figure skaters—the one they watched every Thursday, the three of them curled up on the couch.

It made his chest throb. He felt empty. He felt forlorn.

He felt the overwhelming need to shred something.

"Whoa there." Robert stuck his wet nose inside JR's ear. "Ease up, buddy."

"Hey!" JR shook him off. Only then did he realize he had Pie's dirty blue blanket clamped between his teeth.

"Maybe I could have that back?" Pie whispered, wide-eyed.

JR dropped the blanket and pushed it toward Pie. "Sorry."

"Look, you gotta pull yourself together," Robert told him. "The last thing you want to do right now is—"

Just then, there was a shriek. Or rather, two shrieks. One was a human cry of surprise. And the second sounded like nothing JR had ever heard before. It was part scream, part howl, part siren.

Moments later, something furry and grey flew across the room, raining water down on their heads.

"What the—" Robert looked up, but the soggy comet had already passed by.

"Kisa!" Nadya burst out of the washroom, her shirt drenched in soapy water. "Where is she?"

"On the mantel!" JR pointed with his snout. But by the time the other dogs turned, Kisa had already moved on, launching herself up, up, up onto the very top of the bookshelf, some seven feet above the floor.

"Wow!" Pie cried. "Look at her fly!"

Kisa stopped on top of the bookshelf to catch her breath. Soaking wet, she was little more than two big blue eyes, a small nose, and some very sharp claws. For a few moments, she just stood there, shivering like a Chihuahua in Siberia. Then she drew a deep breath, rolled her eyes to the ceiling, and wailed, "What kind of an *idiot* gives a cat a bath?"

"George!" Nadya shouted. "George, help!" She stepped toward the bookshelf, soapy arms outstretched. "Come, Kisa. Don't be scared. Come down."

"Not likely!" Kisa cried, skittering backward. "Is she *crazy*?" she asked the dogs.

"Hey!" JR barked. "Don't call Nadya crazy!"

"You're a dirty stray," Beatrix added. "You *needed* a bath."

"Did not!" Kisa retorted. "I keep myself clean."

"Humph." Beatrix gave the dogs a knowing look. "Fleas," she mouthed.

"I saw that!" Kisa cried. "And I don't have fleas!" She shook herself hard. "Cats don't need baths. Even my old humans knew that."

"What's going on?" George stomped into the living room, still wearing his sailboat pyjamas. "And why is there a squirrel on the bookshelf?"

"Boom!" Robert declared. "Nice one, Georgie!"

"It's Kisa," Nadya said impatiently. "Please get her down. She's scared, and I can't reach her."

"That's a cat?" George squinted up at Kisa, who hissed back. "Oh, okay. C'mere, kitty." He walked over to the shelf and stretched his long arms toward her. "There's nothing to be afraid— Ow!" he cried as Kisa sank her claws into his arm. He pushed her toward Nadya, who hugged her to her chest, then turned and marched off to the bedroom.

George stood for a moment, gazing after them, and JR trotted over to join him. He leaned against his ankles in a show of solidarity. But George just sighed and nudged him away, following Nadya into the bedroom.

JR turned back to the dogs. Robert and Beatrix were shaking their heads. Pie was mauling his toenail.

"George isn't going to stand for this," JR told them, putting on his bravest face. "I can tell. We're on the same page here."

"Uh-huh." Robert sounded doubtful. Beatrix frowned. Pie didn't look up from his toenail.

"Seriously," JR insisted. "This won't last."

But even as the words left his mouth, he knew he was dead wrong.

5
Praha

First Kisa had to be dried off and fed. Then all the humans had to shower. And then, after all the dogs had eaten breakfast and Pie had gone out to do his business one more time, and George had donned his favourite summer scarf and doused himself in his new cologne ("It smells like bergamot, boy! Not sure what that is, but they say it's manly."), they were finally ready to leave.

"Let's get a move on, everyone," John said, snapping leashes on Robert and Pie. "I think we all need to get out of the apartment."

JR couldn't agree more. Most of all, he needed to get away from the apartment's newest tenant, who was settling in far too quickly. She'd just claimed one of the couch cushions for a bed and was snoring soundly.

She'd mentioned having humans, so she obviously hadn't been born a stray. Had she left

them for a reason? he wondered. Or had they gotten rid of her? But as curious as he was, he wasn't
about to ask. Just the thought of talking to a cat
made his toes curl and his ears tingle and—

"Easy, buddy," Robert said, joining him at the
front door. "You're doing it again."

JR realized that he was grinding his leash
between his teeth. He dropped it. "Right."

"You just gotta try not to think about her,"
said Robert.

JR gave himself a good shake, but he couldn't
help stealing another glance at the sleeping cat.
What might she do while they were out? What if she
took over his bed? What if she stole his biscuits?

"Snap out of it, J!" Robert thumped him on the
nose. "We're in Praha! The land of dumplings and
goulash and ..." He paused. "Well, who knows what
else! Let's explore this place and deal with the floor
mop later."

"He's right, JR," Beatrix said, allowing Nadya
to fasten a leash to her rhinestone-studded collar.
"Forget about her for now. When we get back, we'll
put our heads together and decide what to do."

"Okay." JR sighed, though he wasn't sure it
was possible to forget about Kisa. "Let's go."

They headed for the river, the humans following the map in John's guidebook and the dogs
following the scent of mud and wet grass. According
to JR's nose, the Vltava wasn't the cleanest river,

but it would do for an afternoon dip if the sun got too hot. Already it was high in the cloudless sky.

"It's a perfect day for a long walk," Pie said, trotting alongside him.

"Yeah." JR tried but failed to muster some enthusiasm. He focused on breathing in the smells of Prague and not shredding his leash.

Apparently, the river was the place to be in the morning. The banks on either side bustled with people; some were in business clothes, headed to work, but most were just out for a stroll in the sun.

"John was right. Praha does love dogs!" Robert exclaimed, giving a passing German shepherd a good sniff. A pair of bichons trotted by, nodding hello, followed by a Great Dane loping alongside its jogging human.

"Wow." JR craned his neck, looking around. "Dogs are everywhere!"

"Unfortunately, so is their business." Beatrix wrinkled her nose as she sidestepped a fresh pile of it.

George, unfortunately, wasn't so lucky. "Darn it!" he cried, hopping on one foot. "Don't people pick up after their dogs?"

"That's the one downside to Praha," Nadya said while George tried to wipe his shoe on the pavement. "Though the Czechs love their dogs, they don't often pick up after them. But they say that stepping in it is good luck," she added brightly.

John made a face. "If that's good luck, I'd hate to see what counts as bad."

They walked on along the river, greeting some short-haired pointers, a Shih Tzu, and a trio of retrievers. Robert bounded up to introduce himself to each one. Normally, JR would have been right beside him, but today he couldn't find the energy. He offered a few nods, just to be polite.

"There it is!" John cried. "Charles Bridge! Come on." He pulled them all onto a big stone bridge, lined on either side by black statues and tall lanterns. The bridge was teeming with people: tourists snapping photos of the statues and each other, musicians busking for spare change, and artists hawking their sketches to passersby. JR's ears rang with the sounds of fiddles and accordions and a dozen different languages.

"Yikes!" He ducked to avoid a swinging camera and dodged a stroller just before it ran over his paws.

"This is terrifying!" Pie squeaked, gluing himself to John's trousers.

John himself didn't seem bothered. In fact, he still hadn't looked up from his guidebook. "The statues lining the bridge are hundreds of years old," he read aloud. "And most of them were built to honour saints."

"Hey, look at this one over here!" Robert led them over to a statue of a man with a halo of stars around his head. At its base, a bronze relief showed a soldier petting a dog. Unlike the rest of the carving, the dog was golden, as if someone had rubbed it till it shone. And sure enough, as they stood there, a young man slipped between them and the statue to touch the dog's head. Then he straightened and grinned at the humans. "It's good luck," he explained, then walked away, whistling.

"Dogs are good luck in Praha!" Robert cheered. "This city's the best!"

"They do that in Moscow, too," JR reminded him, thinking of a statue in a Moscow metro station that honoured a dog who'd been killed on a train. People rubbed that one for good luck, too.

Robert gave him a tired look. "A little enthusiasm wouldn't kill you, J."

JR sighed again. "Okay, okay."

They wandered on, past more statues and more musicians, weaving around vendors selling puppets and fudge and chess sets. By the time they reached the other side, JR's senses were spinning.

"Ugh." George winced as a busker blared a French horn in his ear. "Can we get away from here? I've had enough of this crowd."

JR had to agree. Even Robert was looking a little dizzy.

"Is there a park on the way up to the circus?" John asked. "Somewhere we can sit for a while?"

Nadya thought for a moment, then nodded. "I know just the place. It's part of the castle grounds, and always quiet and shady."

"Sounds perfect," said John.

Nadya steered them onto a side street heading toward Prague Castle.

"That's more like it." Beatrix tossed her head. "All those sweaty humans were making my hair frizzy."

JR took a deep breath to calm his nerves, then froze as a waft of butter and sugar flooded his nose. "Whoa," he said. "Smell that?" He whirled around to find the source, only to see George pressed up against a shop window, peering down at a table crammed with cakes, cookies, and tarts.

"This must be one of the famous Czech cake shops." John whistled.

Nadya nodded. "They call this a *cukrárna*."

"And I call it snack time!" said George.

Five minutes later they were back on the street, munching on pastries as they strolled.

"More points for Praha!" Robert declared, and this time, JR agreed. Or rather, he would have had his mouth not been full of cookie. "What could be better than—" Robert stopped, mouth open, when the woods came into view.

"Welcome to Stag Moat," said Nadya.

"Goodness!" Beatrix exclaimed.

"Crikey," said Robert.

Pie could only whimper.

JR swallowed his cookie and licked his lips.

Now *this* was a park.

Actually, it was more than a park. Even the nicest city parks JR had known were grassy and manicured, like Letna Park. Stag Moat, however, was tangled and weedy and overgrown and just the way a park should be. Enormous trees covered in creeping ivy shaded them from the sun. A skinny creek ran alongside them, and dirt paths snaked up the banks on either side. It was practically a forest, right in the heart of the city.

JR's hind legs began to tremble.

"Stag Moat, which surrounds the castle, was at one time a natural defence from invaders," John read from his book. "It was named for the deer that used to inhabit it, and even bears once lived here!"

"Off-leash! Off-leash! Off-leash!" Robert chanted, his tail whipping around like a propeller. Beatrix pranced on the spot.

"Let's sit down awhile," Nadya suggested, leading the way to an enormous poplar tree. The humans spread out their jackets and sat down underneath it.

"You won't go anywhere, will you, boy?" George asked, and JR returned his most innocent

look. George let go of the leash, turning his full
attention to the marzipan cookies he'd bought at
the *cukrárna.*

JR forced himself not to make a break for it—
at least not right away. He'd wait until something
squeaky popped out of the bushes. His Terrier
Senses told him there were hundreds, if not thousands, of squeaky things around.

In the meantime, he explored the ground for
intriguing scents, of which there were thousands.
He picked up an excellent one—rotten and smoky
with a hint of mushroom—and began to follow it,
nose pressed firmly in the dirt. It led him to the
base of a gnarled old tree, which he circled, hoping
that on the other side he might come snout to
snout with—

He stopped short when he saw them.

Cats.

A pair of skinny tabbies looked up in surprise,
then hissed at him. One unsheathed her claws and
took a swipe.

"Hey!" JR jumped back.

The cats shrieked with laughter.

"Scaredy-dog!" one yelled.

"Poor little puppy!" the other chimed in.

JR collected himself and bared his teeth, but
it was too late. They'd seen his weakness. Smelled
his fear.

Suddenly, the entire forest was ringing with calls of "scaredy-dog!" and shrieks of laughter. They were everywhere.

The sun slipped behind a cloud and the woods darkened as the cats yowled and cackled. JR scuttled backward, toes curled and heart pounding. He felt like George gazing out a third-floor window.

He turned tail and ran.

"What's going on?" Robert called as he passed, but JR didn't stop until he'd reached his human.

"Hey, boy!" George scooped him up and plopped him on his lap. He ruffled JR's ears with a big, warm hand that smelled like marzipan. "Whoa, you're shaking! What's wrong? What'd you see over there?"

If JR could speak Human, he would have replied, "Our future, you lunkhead. And it's terrifying."

6
Circus Sergei

"Prague Castle has been around since the ninth century!" John informed the group as they toured the enormous castle grounds. "Imagine! Bohemian kings, Roman emperors, and Czech rulers have lived here for over a thousand years!"

They'd spent the past hour admiring the turreted churches, elaborate gardens, and towering red-roofed palaces that made up the castle complex. They'd stopped to watch the changing of the guard at the gate and a string quartet performing in a courtyard. It was every bit as stately and beautiful as John's guidebook had promised.

And JR hated every inch of it. He was completely, utterly *done* with Prague.

"I think I was destined to live in a palace," Beatrix said, nodding at a passing guard as if he were a servant fetching her kibble.

"It'd be pretty sweet to have humans waiting on you hand and paw," Robert agreed. "I could live with that."

"I don't know." Pie stared up at a statue of a soldier riding into battle. "I think I'd be scared to live in a place this big."

"It's just a bunch of old buildings," JR grunted. "Nothing to be afraid of. Seriously, Pie, you're worse than George."

"Hey now," Robert warned him. "That's my brother you're talking to."

"Sorry," JR muttered, though he wasn't really. All he wanted was to be at home in bed. At home in bed in *Moscow.*

"You're grumpy," Beatrix observed. "And it's not doing anyone any good. I told you, we'll deal with the cat later. Just relax and enjoy the scenery."

JR wanted to retort that that was easy for her to say. Half the stray cats in Prague hadn't just called her "scaredy-dog." Nor did she have one of them vying to be part of her family. But there was no use in arguing with Beatrix, especially when she was pretending to be a princess.

They left the castle grounds and climbed even higher up the hill, until they once again found themselves at the lookout in Letna Park.

"Prague is an inspiration." Pie sighed, gazing out over the city. He closed his eyes, likely composing his poem.

JR watched a riverboat churning slowly down the Vltava. "Meh," he said. Robert gave him a tired look.

"Hey look!" George pointed behind them, and they all turned. A few hundred feet away, a half-dozen red-and-white tents stood where yesterday there had only been grass. "You were right," he told Nadya. "The circus *did* spring up overnight!"

"Come on!" Nadya led them over to the tents, which were still being set up. A cluster of children watched nearby, whispering and giggling.

"This is bringing back memories." Nadya smiled at the children. "Growing up, Niko and I would practically live at the circus whenever it came through our town. Come, let's go find him and Masha."

The grounds were buzzing with action. Workers hauled on ropes and hammered stakes into the grass, securing the tents in place. A group of dancers jetéd by, chased by some tailors with measuring tapes and jugglers tossing pins in the air.

"Crikey!" Robert's head swivelled this way and that. "This place is crazy!"

"It's fascinating," said Beatrix.

Pie just whimpered, his eyes practically bulging out of his head.

Suddenly, George gasped, and JR turned to see a pair of clowns in baggy trousers and white face paint, rehearsing a routine nearby. All thoughts of stray cats disappeared as his Terrier Senses kicked into action. He scampered over to calm his human.

Nadya turned to George in disbelief. "You are *not* afraid of clowns, too," she said.

George tugged on his scarf. "Maybe."

"Look, there's Niko." John pointed, and they turned to see him strolling their way, dressed in a red track suit. JR gave George's trouser leg a firm tug—now was not the time for a clown-induced panic attack.

"What an interesting world you live in, Niko," John marvelled, pulling out his camera and snapping a photo of the clowns.

Niko shrugged, clearly not as impressed. "Would you like to watch a rehearsal?" he asked.

"Absolutely," said John. "Shall we tie up the dogs?"

Niko looked down at them, and the dogs tried to look as harmless as possible. He shrugged again. "They're on-leash. Bring them along."

"We get to see a rehearsal!" Pie gasped. "It's a dream come true! I might faint."

"Keep your fur on, Pie," Robert said, nudging him after the humans. "And no howling, no matter how much you like it. Got it?"

"I'll try," Pie whispered, trembling from nose to tail.

They followed Niko to the big top and quietly slipped in through a side door. Inside, rows of benches circled a centre ring. Most were empty, except for one at the very front, where Sergei sat, still dressed in his old, rumpled blazer.

"Look, it's the director!" Pie squeaked, trying to get a good look.

Beatrix shushed him.

"This way." Niko steered them to the opposite end of the ring.

They sat down a few rows back—humans on the benches and dogs at their feet. Sergei, focused on the action in the ring, didn't seem to notice them. Once JR was settled, he turned his attention there, too.

"Whoa!" he exclaimed, forgetting to be quiet at the sight of a most peculiar animal. About three feet tall and covered in black hair, it had long, lanky arms and enormous ears. "What is *that*?"

"That's a chimpanzee," Beatrix informed him. "I saw one on the nature channel Johanna watches."

"Huh. Was it dressed in a getup like that?" Robert nodded at the ape's costume, a little white suit with a red flower in its lapel.

Beatrix shook her head. "Definitely not."

"Is he ..." Pie cocked his head to the side. "Is he *dancing*?"

As they watched, the chimp took the hand of a woman in a matching white dress. She twirled around him, and he did a clumsy little soft-shoe.

"If you can call it that," Beatrix said dubiously.

"Hey, he's a chimp," Robert said. "He's not supposed to dance."

"Still." Beatrix sniffed. "He has no rhythm."

"I think he's magnificent," Pie breathed.

JR squinted at the strange scene. He'd never met a chimp before, so he couldn't say for certain, but he was fairly sure this one wasn't particularly enjoying the routine. His jazz hands seemed rather half-hearted.

Eventually, Sergei rose and stopped the dance. He gave the woman some pointers, then waved them off, returning to his chair.

Niko grumbled something under his breath, but JR couldn't catch it.

Sergei clapped his hands, and a moment later a clown appeared, tugging the leash of an even *stranger* creature. It was tall and thin up top, but hefty on the bottom, with enormous feet. And it leaped like a giant, upright rabbit.

"What the heck is *that*?" JR asked.

"It's a kangaroo!" Robert exclaimed. "We've got loads of 'em back home, don't we, Pie?"

"Except back home they don't wear boxing gloves." Pie cocked his head to the side. "Do you think that's a Czech thing?"

"Huh?" Robert and JR turned back to the ring, where the clown was helping the kangaroo into a pair of boxing gloves. As they watched, the clown took a few swings at the animal, and she reluctantly swung back. The clown pretended to get knocked down flat, and JR could have sworn he saw the kangaroo roll her eyes.

"I don't know if I like this," George murmured.

"It is weird to see a wild animal in boxing gloves," John agreed.

"No, I meant that clown." George shuddered.

"I can't believe you're afraid of clowns, too." Nadya sighed.

"It's called coulrophobia," George replied defensively. "And it's a real condition."

Niko grunted, but JR couldn't tell what was disturbing him the most—George's condition, the boxing kangaroo, or the old director, who had once again stood up to stop the performance.

"What's he saying?" John asked.

"The clown wanted to try something new," Niko replied. "And Sergei didn't like it."

JR watched the kangaroo take it all in with dull eyes. He'd never met a kangaroo before either, but he would have bet his weight in biscuits that this one wanted to clock both humans in the nose.

"Wow," Robert whispered after the clown and kangaroo had left the ring. "This circus thing is weird."

"I agree," Beatrix said. "I don't like it."

"I think it's amazing," Pie declared, and they all turned toward him. His eyes, still the size of supper dishes, stared unblinking at the ring. "In fact, I think I've found my destiny."

"Hold on, Superstar. Not so fast." Robert held up a paw. "Or Sergei'll have you in a tutu with a monkey riding on your back."

"I'm serious." Pie turned to face them. "Maybe the circus needs a spoken word performance. I have that new poem, remember?"

"'Stopping by the Dog Park on a Snowy Evening'?" JR gave Robert a sidelong look.

"Exactly." Pie nodded, took a deep breath, and then began:

Whose scent this is, I think I know.
He left his business in the snow—

Suddenly Niko stood up. "I think we've seen enough," he announced, and gestured for the humans to follow him.

"Oh, but I want to stay and watch!" Pie whimpered.

"Hush, Pie. Come on." John tugged on his leash.

"But ..." Pie pulled back.

"Heel." John gave his leash a yank, and Pie had no choice but to follow.

Niko led them back outside into the sun and away from the big top, pointing out the costume tent, the ticket tent, and the food tent. Then he led them over to a small barn-like structure, which looked like it might fall over in a good gust of wind. JR took a big sniff, and his senses flooded with feathers and fur, hay and seeds, dust and droppings. He didn't need Niko to tell them they'd found the animal barn.

"Take a look." Niko slid the door open. The dogs squirmed to the front of the group.

When JR's eyes had adjusted to the darkness inside, he found himself staring up into the enormous eye of an elephant, which peered down at them over the door of its stall.

"Is that an elephant?" George exclaimed.

The elephant gave George a tired look.

Niko nodded and stepped inside. JR tried to follow, but George tugged him back.

"The chimp and kangaroo are in here as well," Niko said as he walked down the aisle between their stalls. "Also a goose, some parrots, and—" He froze.

"What?" Nadya asked. "What is it?"

"The most elusive creature of all," Niko said dryly, pulling open the door to the elephant's stall. A moment later, Masha slipped out, red-faced.

"Masha!" Nadya cried. "What were you doing in there?"

"Checking the elephant's foot," Masha admitted, avoiding her father's gaze.

"Masha." Niko shook his head. "You know how Sergei feels."

"But I—" she began.

"No buts."

Masha pursed her lips, then turned to Nadya. "I want to help take care of the animals," she said. "But Sergei doesn't want me to."

"So I heard," said Nadya.

"He wants me to focus on dancing and gymnastics," Masha went on, balling her fists. "And I *hate* dancing and gymnastics!"

Nadya put her arm around her niece's shoulder. "Well, then you shouldn't have to do them," she said.

"Try telling that to Sergei," Niko said, herding them all back outside. "He thinks that Masha could be the next tightrope walker. We haven't had one since ..." His voice trailed off, and he and Nadya exchanged a look.

"Yipes!" said George. "I don't blame you for not wanting to do that. It sounds scary. And dangerous."

But Masha shook her head. "I'm not scared. I just don't want to do it. But I know I could," she added, drawing herself up tall. "Sergei says the talent runs in the family."

"I think that concludes our tour," Niko said abruptly, putting both hands on his daughter's shoulders. He steered them all toward the main exit and sent his visitors home.

On their way back down the hill, George turned to Nadya. "Is Masha's mother still a tight-rope walker?" he asked.

"Oh yes," said Nadya. "She's very good. She performs all over the world—she'll be in Beijing one week and Barcelona the next. That's why Masha lives with Niko—at least she has a caravan to call home."

"Who does her mother perform with?" asked John.

Nadya sighed. "Circus Magnificus."

"No way!" exclaimed George.

"Well, that explains a lot," said John.

Nadya nodded. "Niko was very hurt when she left to chase a flashy, well-paying job." She slipped her arm through George's. "You heard what he said last night—he loves the Old World tradition of a troupe like Circus Sergei. I can't imagine what he'll do if it fails."

"And it's not looking great, is it?" said John. Nadya shook her head and sighed again.

JR thought about the circus all the way home. By the time they reached their apartment, his Terrier Senses were buzzing. Niko and Masha had more problems than he'd realized. He wanted to help them, though he wasn't sure how.

But as they stepped through the door, he was hit with the sour, musky, disgusting scent of *cat*. And just like that, all thoughts of the circus disappeared.

He had his own problems to deal with.

7

Balancing Act

"Well, I for one am beat," George announced, pulling off his shoes and tucking them into the closet so the dogs couldn't reach them. "Anyone else need a nap?"

"Absolutely," John said, wiping sweat off his forehead with his sleeve. "All that fresh air and sun is exhausting."

"Let's have a late dinner and relax until then," Nadya suggested. She scooped Kisa—still sleeping, hours later—off her pile of blankets. "I'm going to read a book in bed." And she slung the lazy creature over her shoulder and headed to the bedroom.

JR's jaw dropped. Nadya was going to allow the cat on the bed? He was *never* allowed on the bed, not even after he'd had a bath! He turned to George to protest the injustice.

But George was too busy trying to untie his summer scarf to notice.

JR cleared his throat.

"What's up, boy?" George finally freed himself from the scarf and looked down.

JR returned a pointed stare.

"Ah." George snapped his fingers. "You want an after-walkie biscuit, don't you? You deserve it, boy."

JR sighed. Humans.

Still, he wouldn't say no to a biscuit. He followed George into the kitchen.

"I'm calling a team meeting," Beatrix announced when he returned. "Meet at the fireplace in two minutes. I'll tell the shepherds."

JR nodded, relieved. If anyone could restore order to a situation like this, it was Beatrix.

He took his place next to the fireplace and waited for the others to arrive and settle in. Beatrix was just calling them to order when Kisa wandered out of Nadya and George's bedroom.

"Hey, dogs." Kisa yawned, stretching one hind leg and then the other. "What's shedding?"

"What's what?" said Robert.

"Get it? Shedding?" She grinned. "I would have said, 'what's shaking?' but you dogs are always shedding."

Pie started to chuckle, but Beatrix stopped him with a glare. "That's not funny," she told Kisa.

Kisa smoothed a whisker. "It's funny if you have a sense of humour."

"Look, we're kind of busy here," JR cut in.

"What's up?" Kisa asked. "You all look so serious."

"It is serious," Pie told her. "We're having a team meeting."

"Quiet, Pie," said Robert.

"It's nothing," JR told Kisa. "We're just talking."

"I like talking," said Kisa. "Can I join you?"

"Sure, why—"

"No," Beatrix cut Pie off.

"It's dog talk," JR told her. "You wouldn't understand."

"Oh." For a moment Kisa looked disappointed. Then she flicked her tail carelessly. "Well, I'm headed for the kitchen. Anyone want anything?"

Pie licked his lips. "I'd like some leftover—"

"No." Beatrix cut him off again.

Pie began mauling his toenail.

"Suit yourself." Kisa sashayed off to the kitchen.

"All right," Beatrix said once she was safely out of earshot. "First order of business: what to do about the cat? Let's brainstorm."

Pie bit his lip. "I don't like storms."

"It's not a real storm," Robert told him. "We're just tossing around ideas. Ask yourself what we should do about the cat, then say anything that comes to mind. In a brainstorm, there are no bad ideas."

"How about we throw her a welcome party?" Pie suggested.

"Except that one," said Beatrix. "That's a bad idea."

Pie turned back to his toenail.

"We could just ignore her," Robert offered.

"Or we could get rid of her," said Beatrix.

JR opened his mouth to agree, then paused as a picture of Nadya popped to mind. Would she be upset if Kisa disappeared? He didn't want to upset her. And yet—

Beatrix gasped.

"What?" They all turned to find her staring up at something on the other side of the room. JR and the shepherds followed her gaze, then gasped as well.

Somehow, without their noticing, Kisa had climbed back on top of the bookshelf, where she'd sought refuge that morning. But this time, she wasn't staying put. As they watched, she bounded from one shelf to the next, then took a great leap and soared across the room, landing lightly on the rim of a tall floor lamp.

"Wow," said Robert.

"Look at her go!" said Pie. "That's impressive."

"It would be if she wasn't a cat," said JR. But even he had to admit Kisa had excellent balance.

Kisa paused only a moment before she was in the air again, now aiming for the mantel above their heads. But this time, she landed slightly off balance, knocking a fancy plate off its stand.

"Look out!" JR dove out of the way just as the plate came crashing down. It hit the floor right beside his bed and shattered into a dozen pieces.

"Hey!" JR whirled to face Kisa, who had hopped down to the floor beside him. "Are you crazy? You could've killed us!"

"Sorry," Kisa said, smoothing out her whiskers. "I usually don't miss like that."

"I could have gotten shards in my hair!" Beatrix turned on her as well. "Do you know how long it takes to get those out?"

"Okay, okay, settle down," Kisa said. "I said I was sorry."

"Sorry isn't good—"

"What happened?" George yelled, running out of the bedroom with Nadya right behind him. "What was that noise?" He stopped short when he saw the broken plate. "Oh no."

"What's wrong?" John jogged out of his own bedroom. "Is everyone okay?"

"Well, I'm glad *someone's* thinking of our well-being," Beatrix huffed.

"I think the dogs broke the plate," George said, kneeling down beside the pieces.

"What?" the dogs all cried at once.

"We didn't do it!" Robert protested.

"How *dare* he?" Beatrix spat.

JR stared long and hard at George, trying to tell him what should have been obvious—that the plate had fallen from the mantel, which none of them could reach.

"Ah well, it's just a plate," said John. "The most important thing is that no one's hurt."

"I love John," Pie whispered, going to lie at his human's feet.

"Oh!" Nadya exclaimed. "Poor Kisa! Look how frightened she is." She scooped up the guilty creature and rocked her in her arms. "That big noise scared you, didn't it?"

"If you don't bite that woman's ankle," Beatrix murmured to JR, "I'm going to do it myself."

"Come, Kisa." Nadya turned and headed back to the bedroom. George watched them go, looking put out. Then he sighed and began to pick up the pieces.

JR watched him for a moment, then turned back to his friends. "I think we've brainstormed enough," he said. "I say we get rid of her."

JR woke with a start sometime around midnight. At least, he figured it was around midnight. The dogs had all gone to bed early, exhausted from their exploring. But he hadn't been asleep long, of that he was certain. So why had he woken up?

Because something was wrong.

He didn't know what, but he knew it for sure. Just like he knew when George was approaching the apartment door after work, even before he heard the jingle of keys. His Terrier Senses were buzzing.

He raised his head and looked around. An almost-full moon shone through one of the windows, illuminating the living room furniture and the shapes of sleeping dogs. There was Beatrix, a giant, shimmering mound on her faux-fur bed. And there was Robert, paws twitching in his sleep. And beside him was Pie's bed.

Empty.

JR leaped to his feet. Where was Pie? He turned in a circle, but couldn't see the shepherd anywhere.

He took a deep breath and told himself not to panic. Pie had probably sneaked into John's room to sleep with him. Yes, that must be it.

Just to make sure, he tiptoed down the hall and nosed open John's bedroom door. Inside, John was snoring, cocooned in his duvet. But his was the only body on the big king-sized bed. JR darted around the room, checking every corner. Pie was nowhere to be seen.

Trembling now, he ran back out to the living room, then paused and closed his eyes. He smelled long and hard, trying to pick up the scent of a timid Australian shepherd. When he finally opened them, he knew one thing without a doubt.

Pie was not in the apartment.

"Guys! Guys, wake up!" he whispered, head-butting Robert and Beatrix each in turn.

"My beauty sleep," Beatrix moaned, burying her snout in her bed.

"Where's that sheep?" Robert leaped to his feet. "Let me at 'im!" He blinked when he saw JR. "Huh?"

"Wake up," JR repeated. "You too, Bea. We've got an emergency."

"Is it the cat again?" Beatrix raised her head. "If it is, I'll pound her into next week."

"Pie's gone."

"What?" Robert yelped. "Where is he? Where'd he go?" He spun in several tight circles, then had to sit down, dizzy.

JR shushed him. "Don't panic, but I've checked everywhere. Pie's not in the apartment."

"Crikey!" Robert leaped up again, then took off down the hallway. Moments later, he returned, wild-eyed. "He's not in the apartment."

"Clearly." Beatrix settled down on her haunches. "Now calm down so we can figure this out."

"Figure what out?" someone asked. They all turned to see Kisa slinking soundlessly across the living room. Her fur gleamed silver in the moonlight.

"Nothing." JR turned away, trying not to think about how she was spending the night snuggled up with George and Nadya. Hopefully she'd sharpened her claws on George's thigh.

"What are we going to do?" Robert whimpered. "Where could he have gone?"

"What's wrong?" Kisa sat down on the floorboards.

"And *why*?" Beatrix asked. "Do you think someone took him?"

"A dognapper!" Robert cried. "Like that guy who stole the stray dogs in Moscow, remember?"

JR swallowed hard. Of course he remembered—he'd helped solve that mystery himself. But this was different, he was sure of it. "Pie went to bed with the rest of us," he pointed out. "Someone would've had to come into the apartment to take him. We would have heard that."

Kisa began to speak again, but Beatrix cut her off. "That's right," she said. "Dogs don't miss a thing."

"Oh Pie." Robert walked over to his brother's bed and flopped down on it. "Where did— Hey, wait a minute." He shoved his nose into the folds of the bed, emerging with a piece of paper clamped between his teeth.

A piece of paper with a muddy paw print on it.

"A note!" JR bounded over. "He left a note!"

"What does it say?" Beatrix asked, joining them. "I'm fluent in Keeshond and Poodle, and I can get by in Schnauzer. But I can't read a word of Shepherd."

Robert squinted at the note, then shook his head. "Doggone it, Pie!"

"What?" JR couldn't stand the suspense. "What does it say?"

"He ran away." Robert sighed. "To join the circus."

JR and Beatrix's mouths dropped open. Then they groaned.

"Great," Robert muttered. "Just great. So what now? And how the heck did he get out?"

"He took the secret passageway," said Kisa.

Three heads whipped toward her.

"The *what*?" asked Robert.

"Don't listen to her," JR snapped, trying not to look at Kisa, whose eerie silhouette was creeping him right out. "She's just a cat."

Kisa flicked her tail. "I might be just a cat," she said, "but I know for a fact that Pie got out through the secret passageway."

"Oh yeah?" JR said. "How do you know?"

"Because I showed him," she replied.

"You *what*?"

"How could you *do* that?" Beatrix cried.

"He could get in trouble out there!" Robert yelped.

"He *will* get in trouble," added Beatrix. "He's Pie."

"I wanted to help him," Kisa said. "He wants to be a performer, and he's actually pretty good. He recited a poem for me—something about a dog park. Spoken word's not really my thing, but I think he has potential."

Robert rolled his eyes. "Well, we gotta go after him. You said there's a secret passageway?"

"You'd better not be lying, cat." Beatrix stepped menacingly toward Kisa.

For a moment, the cat shrank back. Then she drew herself up and returned the stare. "I'm not lying," she said. "I can show you. If you haven't already found it yourself," she added with just a hint of a taunt.

"Of course we've found it," JR said quickly.

Robert and Beatrix both turned to look at him. "You did?"

"Maybe." They stared a moment longer. "Okay, no," he grumbled. "But it can't be that hard to find, if a cat can find it."

"It's not," Kisa agreed. "Come on."

She led them to the hall closet and batted it open with her paw. At the very back, behind a pile of shoes and a few old brooms and dustpans, was another door, open just a crack.

"Where does that go?" Robert whispered.

"To the apartment next door," said Kisa. "No one lives there, but in the back bedroom, there's a window that's wide open and low to the ground." She licked her paw, then cleaned her ears. "At one time, this was probably one big house."

"Wouldja look at that?" Robert marvelled.

"I'm sure we would have found it if we'd looked," JR muttered.

"Come on, team," said Robert. "There's no time to lose."

"Right behind you," said Beatrix. "I'm sure we can retrace our steps back to the circus."

"Hey, can I come?" Kisa asked.

"No," JR replied flatly.

"Why not?" Kisa wrinkled her nose. "I bet I could help."

Robert looked like he was considering it. "Well, maybe. Since you did—"

"Uh-uh," JR cut in. "No way."

"All right, whatever." Kisa stood up, then turned and headed for the bedroom. "Good luck," she offered over her shoulder.

"Let's go," JR said before anyone could rethink it.

And they slipped into the empty apartment.

8
Runaway

You never really knew a city until you'd explored it at night. JR had learned this long ago, since George sometimes had trouble sleeping and would take long walks in the middle of the night.

In Paris, they'd eaten falafel from food carts alongside young Parisians who'd been out dancing all night. In Kuala Lumpur, they'd sampled roti canai at night markets while listening to people sing karaoke.

In Moscow, he'd scarfed down stuffed potatoes in the middle of Red Square. He'd investigated the darkest corners of the Kremlin and met the strays that called them home. He'd even ridden the Moscow metro and explored its fancy station halls.

So when he slipped out of the apartment window and onto the cobblestones under the full moon, he couldn't stop his hind legs from doing a little dance. They were going to see the real Prague, off-leash and at night.

"And find Pie," Beatrix reminded him with a stern look.

He hated it when she read his mind. "I know," he said defensively. Then he turned to Robert. "To the river?"

"To the river."

They headed toward the Vltava, following the same smells of damp earth and muddy water they'd followed just that morning. But now everything felt different, with all the dogs of Prague at home in bed and cool air rising off the water. Most of the humans had gone home, too, except for a few here and there. A cluster of men stumbled by, reliving a soccer game at the top of their lungs. A young couple followed, too busy staring into each other's eyes to care about the men's hollering. They were so besotted, in fact, that the dogs had to leap out of the way to avoid getting trampled.

"John's guidebook was right," Beatrix said as they returned to the path. "Prague is a city for lovers."

No sooner had she said it than another couple approached. Once again the dogs jumped out of their way.

"I've had enough!" the woman was exclaiming. "We're through!"

"Fine by me," the man returned, glaring at the sidewalk. They stomped on by.

"Guess they didn't read the guidebook," JR said, thankful his humans didn't fight like that.

"Can we focus here, please?" Robert snapped. "We've got a runaway to rescue."

"Right." JR and Beatrix hopped back in line behind him.

Robert led them to the now-deserted Charles Bridge, and they ran across it under the dim lantern light and stony glares of the saints. On the other side, they found the street they'd taken earlier and followed it past the *cukrárna* toward Prague Castle.

Suddenly, JR skidded to a halt.

"What now?" Robert asked, sounding exasperated. "What's the holdup?"

"N-nothing," JR replied, but his Terrier Senses were buzzing. Up ahead lay Stag Moat, that beastly forest of felines. Who knew how many cats were slinking around in there, murdering poor, innocent little squeaky things? They were probably watching him from the trees right now, waiting to pounce on his head.

His knees quivered, but he forced himself to stay upright. Now was not the time to pull a Pie. "Hey, g-guys," he said, "maybe we should take a different route."

"What? Why?" asked Beatrix.

"Um, I just think ..." JR thought fast. "We might get lost in the woods. And that would be a big waste of time."

Robert considered this. "I guess so ..."

"Great, c'mon!" JR whirled around and led them away before they could change their minds.

Skirting the woods and the castle grounds, they ran up the hill to Letna Park and paused to catch their breath at the lookout. The lights and spires of Prague stretched below them, flickering like stars under the almost-full moon.

"No time for sightseeing." Robert herded them off toward the tents.

The circus grounds were dark and silent now that the workers had finished setting up and gone home. But JR's Terrier Senses still tingled, telling him the place wasn't quite deserted.

Sure enough, a few moments later his ears pricked up at the sound of a whistle. They all turned to see a night watchman strolling their way, a flashlight swinging at his side.

"Follow me!" JR made a break for the nearest tent. They pressed themselves up against its cool canvas, holding their breath until the whistling watchman had passed.

"If Pie made it this far," Robert whispered once he was gone, "he probably went straight for the barn."

JR sniffed, picking up the musky-sweet scent of elephant. "Come on," he said, leading them past the food tent and the costume tent, then stopping outside the weathered little barn. A light shone through the cracks in the walls.

Robert inspected the front door. "It's shut tight," he reported. "We can't get in."

Beatrix nudged it with her head. "It's flimsy, though. If we all throw our weight against it at once, I bet we could break in."

"Wait. Quiet," JR whispered. He closed his eyes and listened hard. Inside the barn, the animals were talking.

Robert pressed his ear up against the door, paused, then drew back. "It's Pie," he confirmed.

JR and Beatrix pressed their ears up, too.

"This is my very first audition," Pie was saying. "So I'm a bit nervous. And this is a new work. Never before performed."

"Let's have it, then." Someone sighed.

"Uh-oh," Robert whispered.

Pie cleared his throat, then began:

> *I wandered lonely as a dog*
> *in distant lands, with strange new scents*
> *when all at once, in deepest Prague*
> *I glimpsed a host of fire hydrants.*

"We gotta stop this." Robert sprang back from the door. "We're busting in, guys. On my count."

JR and Beatrix leaped to his side and readied their shoulders.

"One ... two ... three!"

They lowered their heads and slammed into the door. It burst open, and they tumbled inside onto the dirt floor.

A half-dozen animals, clustered in the aisle between the stalls, spun around in alarm. The chimp gasped. The kangaroo leaped. A trio of green parrots squawked.

"More dogs?" The elephant peered down at them, looking tired.

"Maybe it's a dancing dog act!" crowed one of the parrots.

"Dogs can't dance," argued the second.

"They can't be worse than the chimp!" The third laughed.

The kangaroo and a snow-white goose snickered. The chimp shrugged, not denying it.

"Don't worry, guys, we're not here to audition." Robert hopped up and gave himself a shake. "We've come to collect our guy. He's got talent, I know. But you can't have him."

"Robert!" Pie exclaimed. "You can't do this! I'm following my dream!"

"Hey now." The chimp held up a furry hand. "Not so fast. This is just the first audition."

"Oh, please ..." Pie turned back to him. "You've got to accept me. I know I'm meant to be onstage with you. Please." He lowered himself to the ground and wagged his tail. The chimp raised an eyebrow at Robert.

"Bro." Robert nudged Pie back to his feet. "Think about it. If you run away to join the circus, there'll be no more lamb kibble. And you *know* how you feel about lamb kibble."

Pie licked his lips. But he shook his head. "I'm sure the meals here are just as good."

"If you like chicken feed," the kangaroo grumbled.

"Day in, day out." The elephant sighed.

Pie closed his eyes. "I'm sure I'll learn to love it. It'll be worth it to be onstage."

"Pie." Beatrix gave him a stern look. "If you run away, you'll have to give up *John*."

Pie's eyes widened. Obviously he hadn't considered this.

"Look, kid." The goose waddled up to him. "I like you. But I'm gonna set you straight. If you're thinking of leaving your cushy life and your human to join this dog-and-pony show, you're nuts."

"Completely crackers!" one of the parrots chimed in.

"Don't do it, kid." The goose shook his head.

"Oh, don't say that," Pie protested. "You're more than a dog-and-pony show."

The goose shrugged. "Dog-and-pony, chimp-and-'roo. You get my drift."

"But you're brilliant!" Pie turned to the chimp. "We saw your routine today. Such spirit! Such grace!"

The chimp scratched his head. "Sure you saw *my* routine?"

"What'd you eat for breakfast, dog?" The first parrot laughed.

"It's Pie," said Pie.

"Well, that explains it," tsked the second parrot. "Dessert for breakfast."

"No, I—"

"Wait a second." JR cut Pie off. "You don't like it here?" He looked from the chimp to the kangaroo to the elephant to the parrots. "*Any* of you?"

The elephant shook his giant head. "I'm sick of carrying humans on my back. They're heavier than they think."

The chimp nodded. "I hate it, too. Contrary to what your friend there thinks, I can't dance. I've got two left feet!" He did a half-hearted shuffle. "Everyone knows chimps don't dance. We swing." And to prove it, he leaped up, grabbed the top bar of the elephant's stall, and began to swing himself up and over it, higher and faster with every turn.

"You're better than the acrobats on the parallel bars!" the elephant told him.

"Don't I know it." The chimp let go of the bar, turned a double flip, and landed square on his feet, long arms outstretched.

"I can't stand boxing." The kangaroo shoved her paws in her pouch. "I'm a lover, not a fighter."

"Now, if Sergei would let you on the trampoline, he'd have a *real* act," said the goose.

"None of us particularly like Circus Sergei," said a low, gravelly voice a few stalls down. JR trotted over and peered inside, only to find himself snout to snout with an enormous orange tiger. He gasped and jumped back, but the tiger just regarded him with sad, dark eyes.

"W-w-what do you do?" JR asked him. "What's your routine?"

"I jump through flaming hoops." The tiger shuddered.

"But he's afraid of fire!" the first parrot squawked.

"He calls it pyrophobia," added the second.

"I told you, it's a real condition!" the tiger protested.

"Hmm." JR looked around. "So ... what would the rest of you rather be doing?"

"We've got an aerial routine," said the first parrot. "With death-defying drops!"

"I'm a contortionist," said the goose. "Mum used to call me the Rubber Chicken. Though clearly I am a goose."

"I don't want to be in the circus at all." The tiger sighed. "It's just not for me."

"Me neither," said the elephant.

"Hmm." JR mulled this over. Once again, his Terrier Senses were tingling. But in a good way this time—the way they tingled when he was coming up with a plan to make everyone happy. He sat down and thought hard.

"Too bad you can't put on a show that shows off everyone's real talents," Robert said. "I bet that'd knock the socks off those Czechs." He paused, then chuckled. "They'd be all like, 'Hey, Czech out this circus!' Get it? *Czech* it out? Ha ha!"

The parrots groaned.

"Hang on." JR looked up at Robert. "Say that again."

"They'd be all like, 'Hey, Czech out this'—"

"Not that part," JR said impatiently. "The part before."

"Oh." Robert cocked his head. "A show that shows off everyone's real talents?"

"Yeah." JR nodded slowly, then faster. "Robert, that's it!"

"That's what?" asked the first parrot.

"What's it?" asked the second.

"What's what?" asked the third.

"You need to put on a show where everyone gets to do what they love!" JR cried. "Think about it!"

The animals all fell silent, thinking.

"It *would* be impressive," Beatrix agreed. "It would probably sell more tickets, too, maybe draw spectators away from Circus Magnificus."

Pie gasped. "It could save the circus!"

"Exactly!" JR cried.

"Except it would never work." The elephant wagged his trunk from side to side.

Everyone turned to him.

"Sergei would never allow it," he explained. "As long as he's in charge, the circus will never change."

"Oh." JR's tail drooped. He'd forgotten about Sergei. "Right."

"Unless ..." said Robert. "Unless Sergei *wasn't* in charge."

"No chance of that," said the chimp. "He'll never step down."

"No, Robert's right!" JR exclaimed, catching on. "What if just once Sergei couldn't make it to the show? And the animals took over."

Everyone fell silent for a minute, imagining it. JR held his breath.

"It's a crazy idea," the kangaroo said slowly.

"Absolutely bonkers," the goose agreed.

"But if it worked ..."

They all fell silent again.

"It could be ..." The kangaroo paused. "The answer to all our problems."

The parrots began to whisper among themselves.

"I'd be willing to ... detain Sergei," the tiger offered.

"I'd help," added the elephant.

Again they all paused. Then the chimp shrugged. "What do we have to lose?"

"Let's do it!" agreed the elephant.

The parrots cheered.

"Good idea, J," Robert commended him.

"I think so, too," he agreed. "But it's going to take some planning." He motioned for everyone to put their heads, snouts, trunks, and beaks together.

For the next hour, they planned it all out. Robert would herd Sergei into the barn, where the elephant and tiger would hold him hostage. Meanwhile, the parrots would put on an aerial show, the chimp would take over the parallel bars, the kangaroo would commandeer the trampoline, and the goose would escape from a straitjacket.

"And I'll perform my poem!" said Pie.

"Right." JR and Robert exchanged a glance. "We'll work on that."

It was going to take a lot of practice. But it was a good plan, JR just knew it. And they'd put it into place on Opening Day, in three days' time.

"What we need now is a new director," the elephant pointed out as the sky began to lighten outside the barn.

All heads turned to JR.

"How about it, dog?" asked the first parrot.

"Who, me?" he gaped.

He'd never thought of himself as a director. But the more he did, the more he liked it. "Wow. Okay. Thanks!"

They bade the animals goodbye and headed for home, with promises to return again the next night. JR led the way, his tail wagging so furiously he couldn't have stopped it even if he tried.

9
Trapped

As soon as the humans left the apartment the next day, JR assumed his new role as director and called a team meeting at the fireplace.

"Where's Pie?" he asked once Beatrix and Robert had settled in.

"Bathroom," said Robert, jerking his head in that direction. "He's practising his monologue."

JR cocked an ear. Sure enough, he could hear Pie humming from the bathroom.

"Vocal warm-ups," Robert explained.

"Let's start without him," said Beatrix. "We've got a lot to discuss, and your humans will only be out for a few hours. They've got that big dinner to prepare for."

John had arranged to meet the Australian Ambassador to the Czech Republic for a fancy din-ner, and he'd invited George and Nadya along. This was good news for George, as it meant his afternoon of sightseeing wouldn't last long.

"Why do we need to go to a museum about cafés?" he'd asked when Nadya had suggested it that morning. "Can't we just go to a café? I really want to try some of those sweet cherry dumplings."

"It's not a café museum. It's the *Kafka* Museum," Nadya had said. "Kafka was a brilliant author. Trust me, it'll be interesting."

George hadn't looked convinced.

"We'll stop for dumplings after," Nadya added.

George went to fetch his summer scarf.

"I'm going to see the famous astronomical clock in the Old Town Square," John announced, turning to Robert and Pie. "Want to come, boys?"

In response, the shepherds flopped over on their sides and pretended to sleep.

"Lazy dogs," John said fondly, stooping to stroke Robert's head. "You'd think they'd been out adventuring all night."

Robert covered a chuckle with a snore.

"All right, let's get down to business," JR began once the humans were out the door. "There are only two more days till the show opens, and we've got a lot of planning to do."

"We'll have to sneak out and head to Letna Park as soon as your humans leave for dinner tonight," said Beatrix.

"Which could be tricky, since there'll still be lots of humans around," Robert added. "Prague isn't like Moscow, where we can just blend in with all the strays."

"Some of us blend in better than others," Beatrix said, filing her nails on the floorboards. "I could never be mistaken for a stray."

Robert and JR rolled their eyes.

"And speaking of my striking appearance," Beatrix continued, "I think Circus Sergei needs a new opening act. Someone to rally the crowd with her good looks and charm."

"Good idea." Robert winked at JR. "But who could we get to do that? Know anyone, J?"

Beatrix glared at him. "I'd do it, Biscuit Brain." She turned to JR. "I was in a kibble commercial as a puppy, you know."

"Um, okay," he said, not because he thought the circus needed a beautiful and charming open-ing act, but because he wanted to keep Beatrix in good humour. She was easier to work with that way.

"Hey, dogs," Kisa said, wandering out of the bedroom. "Where'd everyone go?" She stretched and yawned.

"Sightseeing," said Robert.

"Which you'd know if you didn't nap all day," added Beatrix.

Kisa flicked her tail as if deflecting Beatrix's insult. "What are you guys talking about?"

"Nothing." JR turned his back on her. It never failed. Just when he was starting to feel better, Kisa slunk back into his life. Why couldn't she just disappear?

She lingered nearby, cleaning her paws, but he refused to look at her. "Let's talk about how to trap Sergei," he whispered to his friends, and they bent their heads together to discuss. Eventually, he heard Kisa get up and pad away, but he didn't look up.

They were just debating whether Sergei would fit in the parrots' cage when there was a shout from the kitchen.

"JR! Hey, JR!"

It was Kisa.

"What does that fleaball want?" Beatrix frowned.

"I don't care." JR gritted his teeth. "Ignore her."

"J-Aaar!"

"What?" he yelled.

"I want to show you something!"

JR let out a strangled sigh, then heaved himself up off his bed. He stomped into the kitchen, cursing the cat with every step.

"What? Can't you see I'm—" He stopped when he saw her on the windowsill, flexing her knees.

"Watch this!" she said. And she took a flying leap across the room, landing on a rickety set of shelves where the humans kept their food.

"Look out!" JR cried as the shelf swayed, but Kisa held on until it steadied. Then she began to climb, straight up, past the pasta and the cereal and George's stash of chocolate chip cookies, until she reached the very top shelf. She took a deep breath, found her balance, and tiptoed along its edge, coming to a halt next to JR's dog biscuits.

"Whoa," he said, forgetting to be unimpressed. "How do you do that?"

"Nice, huh?" she said. "It's all in the tail. I couldn't balance without it." And she reached out and tipped over the open bag, showering a dozen biscuits down on JR.

"*Whoa!*" He caught a few and gulped them down, then chased a few more across the tiles. Then he skidded to a stop, remembering that she was the enemy. He couldn't be won over that easily.

And yet, there was no sense in letting the biscuits go to waste.

He scarfed down a few more, then took some back to his bed for later, plus a few to share with Beatrix and Robert, since they'd inevitably ask. He grunted his thanks over his shoulder.

"Anytime," Kisa replied brightly.

JR sensed George and Nadya coming minutes before their key turned in the lock. He ended the team meeting and was just going to greet his humans when his senses lit up, freezing him in his tracks.

He could feel it even before they stepped through the door and confirmed his worst nightmare.

George and Nadya were fighting.

"I'd been so looking forward to seeing the Kafka Museum!" Nadya said, stomping into the apartment. "He's one of my very favourite authors."

"Well, he might write okay books, but he's also crazy!" George retorted, slamming the door behind them.

"Hoo, boy." Robert sat down to watch. "This is gonna be good."

"Kafka was not crazy." Nadya dropped her purse. "He was ..." She thought for a moment. "Eccentric."

"Which means crazy." George tugged at his scarf, stuck inside it again.

JR's stomach lurched. This couldn't be happening. His humans didn't fight. Couples like the one they'd seen near the Vltava fought. Not George and Nadya.

His Terrier Senses were now buzzing out of control. But for once, he had no idea how to make things better.

"What's the matter?" John poked his head out of the bathroom. He'd returned home shortly before to get ready for their night out. Half his face was covered in shaving cream.

Nadya took a big breath, and JR snapped into action, scampering across the living room to her feet. He leaned against her ankles, sending her calming vibes.

"The Kafka Museum is a fascinating place," she began. "It puts visitors in the mind of Franz Kafka—"

"Who was crazy," George added, still wrestling with his scarf.

"Eccentric," Nadya said tersely. "He wrote about some strange things, like men being turned into bugs."

George gave John a knowing look, turning his index finger in a circle around his ear. "Loopy," he mouthed.

Nadya ignored him. "Unfortunately, there are some uncomfortably small spaces at the Kafka Museum. And George, it turns out, is afraid of small spaces."

Robert and Beatrix sighed. JR leaned harder against Nadya's ankles.

"It's called claustrophobia!" George finally freed himself from his scarf and tossed it across the room. "And it's a *real thing!*"

Pie went to hide under John's bed.

JR could sense Nadya counting backward from ten. She walked over to the fireplace and began straightening the dog beds.

"It's a real thing," George insisted to John, who shrugged and returned to the bathroom.

The tension between George and Nadya was making JR's stomach hurt. He had to do something to bring them back together. He had to—

Something clattered to the floor, and all heads turned toward Nadya, who'd been shaking out JR's flannel bed. A half-dozen biscuits now lay scattered at her feet.

"JR!" she cried. "Were you stealing biscuits?"

Stealing! JR jumped. He looked around for Kisa, but she was nowhere in sight.

That doggone cat!

"What?" George marched over to inspect the crime scene.

"This is not going to go well," Beatrix observed.

"JR, you little thief!" George shook his head, staring at the biscuits. "How did you do that? Sneaky!"

JR's ears went hot. Was his human insane? The biscuit box was a good eight feet off the floor. Jack Russells were talented jumpers, but this was ridiculous.

Nadya knelt to scoop the biscuits off the floor, then marched them back to the kitchen. "We need to get ready," she called back to George. "We can't be late."

"I'm never late," grumbled George, who was always late. He wagged a finger at JR, then headed to the bedroom.

With a huff, JR settled back into his bed. Humans were ridiculous creatures.

"At least you didn't get punished," Robert said, settling down beside him.

"Punished!" JR spat, his ears still burning. "For something I didn't even do? That would have been totally unfair." He lay down and put his head on his paws. "Punished. Ha. I'd like to see them try."

"The bathroom? You're locking me in the *bathroom*?"

JR couldn't believe it. He'd never been locked in the bathroom before, not even the time he destroyed the Dumont-Sauvage Seafaring Nomad AC III, George's prized wristwatch.

"I'm sorry, boy," George said as he shut the door. "But it's for the best. If you get into those biscuits again, you could get sick."

The bathroom door closed with a loud, final *click.*

JR scratched at the door. He whined. He even barked. But it was no use. George, Nadya, and John were off to their swanky dinner. He heard the front door close behind them.

He sat down, stunned. This couldn't be happening. Not tonight, when he had to get to the circus grounds for rehearsal. He was the director! He couldn't miss rehearsal!

His head was spinning. His paws were trembling.

He was going to shred something.

Quite possibly something grey and fluffy.

"Stay calm, J," Robert called from the other side of the door. "Deep breaths, buddy. We'll get you outta there."

JR took a shaky breath.

"I don't see how," he heard Beatrix say. "This door's too heavy for us to open."

"Don't worry, JR!" Pie called. "If you get hungry, try the hand towels. They're surprisingly tasty and easy to digest."

JR lay down on the tile with a whimper.

"JR!" another voice called through the door.

It was Kisa.

He leaped to his feet and lunged at the door. "What do *you* want? You're the reason I'm stuck in here!"

There was a pause, then she replied, "No, I'm not. I didn't force you to hide those biscuits in your bed."

JR began to argue, then stopped, for she had a point. He sat back down and ground his teeth.

"Anyway, you can get out through the bathroom window," Kisa said.

JR looked up. The window was indeed open a crack, but it was also a good five feet above his head. "What do you think I am, a greyhound?" he shot back. "I can't reach that!"

"Yes, you can," Kisa said matter-of-factly. He could picture her sitting on the other side of the door, flicking her tail. It annoyed him even more. "Just climb up on the toilet. But try not to fall in."

He heard Robert snort softly.

"That's not funny!" JR yelled.

"It's funny if you have a sense of humour," said Kisa.

Robert snorted louder.

"I heard that!" JR yelled.

"Sorry," said Robert, but JR could tell he was still amused.

"And even if I could get up there," JR continued, "the window's too high off the ground. I could break my legs jumping out!"

"There's a ladder leaning against the wall outside," said Kisa. "Just climb down it."

How did she know all this? JR began to ask, then stopped. It didn't matter: rehearsal was starting soon, and he had to get going.

"We'll sneak out through the other apartment and meet you outside," said Beatrix. "If you're not there in five minutes, we'll have to leave without you."

"Oh, I'll be there," JR grumbled. No stupid cat was going to keep him away from his new job. He licked his lips, bent his knees, then launched himself up on the toilet seat, where he teetered, but didn't fall in. He paused to find his footing, then hopped up on the tank. So far, so good.

From there, it was only a small step up to the windowsill, which was just wide enough for him to stand on. Outside, evening was falling on the courtyard, turning the trees and flower beds golden. He steadied himself on the windowsill, then nosed the window open.

"You can do this," he whispered. And he squeezed himself outside.

"Go J!" Robert called, appearing on the grass below. "Now grab that ladder!"

That was easier said than done. The ladder was a good foot away from the window ledge, itself only a few inches wide. He stretched a leg out, but the ladder was too far to reach. His only option was to jump.

Shutting out the voice in his head reminding him that Jack Russells did not always land on their feet, he leaped for the ladder.

He missed.

The next thing he knew, he was on the grass, staring up at the concerned faces of his friends.

"JR," Pie whispered, nosing him in the ribs. "Are you dead?"

JR rolled over with a groan. "No," he replied. "But that cat's going to be."

10

Dress Rehearsal

"Places, everyone! Places!" JR barked. He nodded at Robert, who trotted over to the barn door and assumed his position as guard, on the lookout for the night watchman.

"Everyone ready?" JR looked at the performers, who were gathered in the aisle between the stalls. The space was a little cramped, but they'd agreed that sneaking into the big top was just too risky.

The three parrots settled on the top bar of the elephant's stall and looked expectantly at JR. He took a deep breath and pushed the last lingering thoughts of Kisa to the very far corners of his brain.

It was time to be a good director.

"A one and a two and ..." He nodded at the parrots.

The birds began humming the strains of the song that always opened the circus. At this point, a beautiful woman in a ball gown would strut into the ring and start serenading the audience. And just as she did, a well-groomed keeshond would march out to upstage her.

Thanks to her kibble commercial, Beatrix knew just how to act in the spotlight. She trotted around, tossing her head and batting her eyelashes at an imaginary audience.

"Consider this show stolen," she told JR as she passed.

"Let's wrap this up," JR whispered to the parrots, who hummed faster to reach the end of the song.

"Okay, good job, Bea," JR shouted. "Time for the first act, everyone. Where's the chimp?"

"Right here." He stepped up, jazz hands at the ready. JR nodded at the parrots, who struck up the next song, and the chimp jogged into the centre of the aisle, pretending to hold the dancer's hand.

He began dancing as he normally would—a sway here, a turn there. But after a few moments, he suddenly threw his arms up and abandoned the act. Then, with a whoop of joy, he ran over to the kangaroo's stall, grabbed hold of the bar, and began his real routine.

The chimp swung higher and faster, twisted and flipped in the air. It was an amazing performance, and it would be even better in the big top, where he could take over the parallel bars.

And best of all, the chimp himself was loving it. His dull eyes now shone with life, and he couldn't stop grinning. He finished with a double flip and a perfect dismount, arms outstretched. The animals cheered, and the chimp took a bow.

"Perfect!" JR shouted. "You're going to bring down the house!" A shiver ran from his nose to his tail. The chimp wasn't the only one loving his new role.

"All right, next act," JR called. "Where's the contortionist?"

"Right here!" The goose waddled over, flexing his wings. "The Rubber Chicken, at your service. Though clearly," he added, "I am a goose."

"Right," JR said, and stepped back to watch. "Let's see it."

The chimp pulled off his suit jacket and proceeded to wrap it around the goose. He swaddled the bird up tight, knotting the jacket arms behind him. Then he carried the bundle over to the centre of the aisle, set it down, and stepped away.

The parrots struck up a tense and ominous tune, and the struggle began. The goose began to wiggle. He stretched his neck out, then pulled it back in. He flipped over on his belly, then back onto his wings. He groaned. He grunted. He grimaced.

"Does he actually know what he's doing?" Beatrix whispered. JR shook his head. He had no idea.

Minutes passed, and still the goose struggled. The parrots were starting to tire of their song. The chimp looked like he wanted to step in and loosen the knots.

But just as JR was about to suggest they rethink the routine, or at least the goose's stage name, the bird burst free of his binds, wiggling out through the neck of the jacket. The animals gasped.

The goose stretched his wings, then honked triumphantly. "The Rubber Chicken, ladies and gentlemen!" he cried, taking a deep bow.

"Oh wow!" JR cried. "That was phenomenal. I've never—"

"Human!" barked Robert, bursting into the barn. "Human approaching! Everyone hide!"

The animals scattered, diving for their respective stalls. Doors slammed shut, and the chimp hit the lights just seconds before the main doors creaked open and a figure slipped in.

JR had leaped inside the closest stall, and now found himself huddled behind one of the elephant's feet. Twice his size, it would certainly crush every bone in his body with one misstep.

"Don't move," he whispered, both to himself and the elephant. "Don't move a muscle."

The visitor paused a moment, then flicked on the lights. The elephant made a show of yawning, as if he'd been asleep all the time.

"I'm sorry to wake you," Masha said in a small voice. "I couldn't sleep."

JR's Terrier Senses lit up. Masha was upset. She needed comforting. But what could he do? If she saw him, he'd be done for.

The elephant's stall door slid open with a groan, and Masha slipped inside. JR dove to the very back corner, burying himself in a pile of straw and hoping it wouldn't make him sneeze.

"I'm sorry," Masha said again, reaching up to stroke the elephant's trunk. "I just need someone to talk to. And you're the best listener."

JR peeked out through the straw and watched the elephant lower his head so Masha could scratch his ear. Her cheeks were wet with tears.

"It's bad news," Masha warned the elephant, then took a deep breath. "Circus Magnificus has been stealing our performers."

JR heard Pie gasp in the next stall. The kangaroo covered it with a cough.

"Three of our best acrobats are quitting Circus Sergei to work for them instead," Masha continued. "Also two clowns. And rumour has it the contortionist is next.

"But that's not all." Masha produced a ball of black satin from under her arm, and shook it out to show the elephant. It was a man's jacket, with a big silver half moon on the back. A familiar-looking half moon. JR squinted at it until he realized where he'd seen it: on the brochure George had brought home from his Circus Magnificus show. "I found this on Papa's bed," she whispered to the elephant, whose eyes widened. "Circus Magnificus wants him, too."

And with that, she burst into tears.

It took all JR's will to stay buried in the straw, though every hair on his body was telling him to go make Masha feel better.

"Papa doesn't want to work for them, and I don't want him to either." She sniffed. "They might send him all around the world, like my mother, and I'll never see him." She wiped her eyes with the jacket, staining the satin with tears. Then she looked up at the elephant. "And if we leave Circus Sergei, I'll never see any of you again either!" She burst into tears once more, and the elephant wrapped his trunk around her and drew her close.

JR closed his eyes and took deep breaths, forcing himself to stay put until Masha's tears subsided. Eventually, she dried her eyes on her sleeve, checked on the elephant's foot, then slipped back out into the night.

After a few minutes, the animals all slunk back out into the aisle, shoulders slumped and heads bowed.

"Did you hear that?" Pie whispered.

"Terrible. Just awful." The goose shook his head.

"What will happen if Niko leaves?" moaned the elephant. "He's the star of the show."

"The circus won't survive," said the tiger.

"And we'll all be separated and sold," whispered the kangaroo.

The animals moaned.

"Wait, guys!" JR held up a paw. "Not so fast. There's still something we can do."

They raised their heads to look at him.

"What?" asked the goose.

He drew himself up as tall as he could. "We can put on a doggone amazing show."

11

Home Wrecker

JR awoke in mid-whimper—paws clenched, ears pricked, heart pounding.

"It was just a dream," he told himself. "It's okay."

But it hadn't been just a dream. It had been a Very Bad Dream.

In it, he'd been directing the circus show, and nothing was going right. The kangaroo sprained her ankle on the trampoline. The chimp forgot his entire routine and froze onstage. Then Sergei escaped his captors and burst into the ring to haul off all the rebellious performers. And JR could only watch from the sidelines, unable to do anything to make it better.

He whimpered again.

"What part of 'beauty sleep' don't you understand?" Beatrix muttered from the bed beside his.

"Sorry," he whispered, blinking hard. Morning light was pouring through the living room windows. After the previous night's excitement, they'd all slept in.

He took a deep breath. "It was just a dream," he said again.

So why wouldn't his paws stop trembling?

Because once again, something was wrong.

He stayed very still, concentrating, until he figured it out.

George and Nadya were fighting again.

He leaped up and made a beeline for the bedroom. The door was open a crack, so he nosed it open wider and slipped inside.

Both of his humans were dressed and ready for the day. Nadya was standing near the bed, fastening the clasp of her necklace. George was staring intently in the mirror, styling his hair so it looked like he hadn't styled it at all.

And there, on the bed, was that darn cat, lolling about like nothing was wrong. Like the silence between George and Nadya wasn't as thick and heavy as a Moscow smog.

JR wanted to grab her by the scruff and shake her. Useless, useless cat.

"Good morning, JR," Nadya said curtly as she left the room. She paused to give him a quick pat, then marched away.

JR turned to George and gave him a long, hard look. George shook his head, still staring into the mirror.

"Don't ask, boy," he said.

This was not good.

JR scampered after Nadya into the kitchen, where John was cracking eggs into a frying pan. Over by the fireplace, the dogs were finally shaking themselves awake.

"Scrambled or over?" John asked Nadya, holding up an egg.

"Scrambled for me," she said.

"And for George?"

Nadya opened the fridge and pulled out a carton of orange juice. "You'll have to ask him yourself."

This was not good at all.

"What are you two planning to do today?" John asked as George joined them in the kitchen. "Any sights you're dying to see?"

Nadya and George exchanged a quick glance, then looked away.

"Well, *I* want very much to see one of Prague's most interesting sights." Nadya poured herself a glass of juice. "The museum in Kutná Hora, just outside the city."

"Sounds good," said John.

Nadya nodded. "But George doesn't want to."

"Because it's a *bone* museum!" George cried. "An old church, all decorated with the bones of dead people!" He shuddered. "That's not interesting. That's *creepy*."

Nadya took a swig of juice, then set her glass down on the counter. "So you're afraid of that, too? A church decorated in bones?"

"Who in their right mind *wouldn't* be afraid of that?" George wailed. "Am I right?" He turned to John, who busied himself with the eggs.

"Did someone say something about bones?" Robert yawned, padding over. "I'm hungry."

"Quiet," Beatrix shushed him, tiptoeing over. "The humans are fighting again. It sounds serious."

"It's not," JR said quickly. "This is nothing. They'll pull through."

But he wasn't so sure. If George and Nadya were dogs, they would have been circling each other, snarling and snapping. He chewed his lip, wishing that George and Nadya actually *were* dogs. Then Nadya would just give George a good, hard bite on the nose to show him who was boss, and they'd get on with things. Humans just had to make everything so *complicated*.

What if ... He swallowed hard, once again picturing the couple on the banks of the Vltava. What if this time ... they *couldn't* pull through?

A whimper escaped him before he could stop it. He sat down on his haunches to think. Before they'd come to Prague, George and Nadya never fought about anything. Now they argued every day. What had changed? Was it Prague? You couldn't very well blame an entire city for making a couple fight.

So what was it, then?

"The cat," he said aloud.

Beatrix and Robert turned to him.

"Come again?" said Robert.

"It's the cat," JR said, nodding as it all began to make sense. "They're fighting because of Kisa. Nadya only pays attention to her these days, and it makes George feel neglected."

Robert and Beatrix exchanged a glance.

"You think so?" Robert asked.

"I know so," said JR.

"Huh." Robert shook his head. "Humans."

"Cats." Beatrix curled her lip.

"What if my family falls apart because of a *cat*?" JR felt sick at the thought. He and George would have to leave Moscow. And move to yet another new city! They'd have to start all over again, just the two of them, friendless and home- less and alone.

He scrabbled over to Nadya and planted him- self right on her feet as she accepted her plate of eggs from John. Leaning against her legs, he sent her his happiest, most calming vibes to remind her how much she loved him and George. She was the best thing that had ever happened to them, despite her inexplicable love of cats. They'd work through that. All was not lost.

He stayed there, warming her ankles, until she nudged him off and slipped away, leaving her uneaten eggs on the counter.

"JR, look!"

JR snarled. He was in no mood to look at anything. Especially something that flea-ridden *home wrecker* wanted to show him. "Go away," he yelled back, and nestled down into his bed.

He'd been lying there since the humans had left a few hours before. Fortunately, John had come up with a new sightseeing plan to suit everyone.

"There's an orchestra playing in the main square," he'd announced after consulting his guidebook. "Let's go take in the show, then eat lunch in an outdoor café."

Nadya and George had both agreed, though somewhat sullenly.

Good old John, JR had thought as the Australian ambassador herded his humans toward the door. He would have made a good terrier, too.

Not a Jack Russell, but something respectable. An Airedale, maybe.

"Should we take the dogs?" George wondered, glancing back at them.

But John shook his head. "Not this time, I think. Last time we took Pie to a concert, he howled all the way through it."

"I was singing along!" Pie protested. "That was my falsetto."

The humans bade the dogs goodbye and left, promising to be back soon.

"C'mere!" Kisa now yelled. "I'm in the spare room."

"I know where you are!" JR hollered back. "And I don't care!" He returned to what he'd been doing for the last few hours: brainstorming ways to make George and Nadya happy again. So far, he hadn't come up with anything good. But he was determined not to leave his bed until he did.

He'd even bowed out of Pie's practice session, although as director, it was his job to help the shepherd improve his performance—especially since Opening Day was just a day away. Now Robert and Beatrix were helping Pie rehearse in John's bedroom. He could hear their muffled voices from the living room, and it only made him feel worse.

Now that he thought of it, his new role and his old one had a lot in common. Both directors and

terriers had to keep everyone happy and everything running smoothly.

"Seriously, you need to see this," Kisa called.

JR ignored her.

"Just this once, then I'll leave you alone!"

JR sighed as loud as he could. "Promise?" he
yelled.

"Promise!"

He heaved himself out of bed and stomped
over to the tiny spare room, which the humans
were using to hang their laundry. "What do you—"
He stopped when he saw her. "Oh no. Not again!"

After the previous day's disaster, George had
moved JR's biscuits to the spare room, once again
about eight feet off the floor, but this time on a
shelf fixed to the wall.

And yet, Kisa had still found a way to reach
them. For Nadya had strung a clothesline from one
side of the room to the other, connecting the shelf
on the wall to a wardrobe opposite it. Now the cat
stood on top of the wardrobe, flexing her knees in
preparation to cross the clothesline.

"You've been pretty grumpy lately, JR," she
said as she tiptoed out onto the line. "But I know
what'll make you feel better!" She paused and batted the line, as if testing its strength. Then she
flipped underneath it and crossed upside down,
hanging on with only her claws.

JR's mouth fell open. "What are you doing?"

"Getting you some biscuits, silly." Kisa flipped right side up and climbed onto the wall shelf.

"No!" JR cried. "I don't want them! You're just going to get me in trouble again!"

Kisa waved off his protests with her tail. "I'll just shake down a few. Come on. You know you want them."

JR's hind legs trembled. He did want them. Very much. But he silenced his stomach and shook his head. "No, I don't."

But Kisa was already tipping the bag over, raining dog biscuits down on the floor.

"Stop it!" JR yelled, skittering after them. "You're making a mess!"

"I can't!" Kisa cried, and he looked up just as the bag slipped out of her grasp and fell to the floor. She tumbled after it, but managed to land on her feet.

"Nooo!" He leaped for the bag, to catch it in mid-air. But he missed, and it hit the floor with a clatter.

Dog biscuits flew everywhere.

"Argh!" JR spun in a circle. The spare room was now a complete mess. George and Nadya were going to kill him. "You did it again! You stupid cat!"

And before he knew it, his Terrier Senses kicked in. But not the good senses this time. The bad senses. The kind that, months ago, had made him destroy the Dumont-Sauvage Seafaring Nomad AC III.

The kind that made him give chase before he could decide whether it was really a good idea.

Before he knew it, he was chasing Kisa out of the spare room. She yowled and ran, but he was in hot pursuit, sprinting down the hallway after her. He heard Robert call out, but he didn't stop. He couldn't stop.

But Kisa was fast and nimble. She faked left, then dodged right for the bathroom. The door was open just a crack—just wide enough for a skinny cat to squeeze through. Unfortunately, it wasn't wide enough for an average-sized Jack Russell terrier. JR hit the door with a smack, then fell backward.

"J!" Robert appeared above him and placed a paw on JR's chest. "Chill out, dude. You've gone full pit bull!"

JR squirmed away and picked himself up, heart still pounding. He shook himself all over, trying to regain control. After a few moments, he turned away from the bathroom and followed Robert back to the spare room, where Pie and Beatrix were feasting on the spilled biscuits.

"Now *this* is an afternoon snack!" Robert bounded over to join them.

"Have some, JR!" Pie called, chasing a biscuit across the floor.

But JR was in no mood for treats. He waited until the dogs had eaten their fill, then began to tidy the place up, pushing the uneaten biscuits under the wardrobe. The squeaky things that lived in the walls were going to have a field day.

"Ohhh," Pie groaned. "I think I'm going to be sick." He headed for his bed in the living room.

Robert sighed after him, then turned to JR. "Hey, J," he said, "think you might have been too hard on the cat?"

"Too hard on the cat?" JR repeated. "Did you see what she did? She's nothing but trouble. I'm so sick of her!"

"Yeah, but—"

"JR did exactly what he had to," Beatrix said, shaking crumbs off her whiskers. "I would have chased her right out of the apartment."

JR gave Beatrix a grateful look. Kisa had deserved a good chase. He didn't regret it one bit.

Well, maybe a *little* bit. But not much. He focused on cleaning up the mess.

Finally, once every treat had either been eaten or tucked away, they joined Pie in the living room.

"Feeling better?" Robert asked him.

Pie nodded. "But maybe we should check up on Kisa," he suggested. "I haven't seen her come out of the bathroom."

Beatrix sniffed.

"Pie's right, J," Robert agreed. "Just tell her she can come out."

JR glowered but gave in. He'd made his point, and now at least she'd leave him alone. He walked over to the bathroom and stood outside.

"Hey," he said. "You can come out now."

Kisa didn't reply, so he nosed the door open and stepped inside.

"Look, I'm not sorry," he told her. "You deserved it. But I'll leave you alone if you—" He stopped and looked around. "Kisa?"

He didn't need his Terrier Senses to tell him, with all certainty, that there was no one in the bathroom.

Nothing but a cool breeze blowing through the open window.

12

Vanished

"That was fantastic!" George proclaimed as he, Nadya, and John burst through the door later that afternoon, reeking of dumplings and sunscreen. "That guy ... What'd you say his name was?"

"Dvořák." Nadya slipped off her jacket and handed it to him.

"That Dvořák." George shook his head, hanging her jacket in the closet.

"Now *there's* a composer."

JR ignored the fact that George couldn't tell a composer from a cocker spaniel and buried his nose in his bed. Normally, he would have delighted in the fact that they were no longer arguing. But now their high spirits were making him feel even worse about the Very Bad Thing he'd done while they were out.

Actually, it wasn't a Very Bad Thing. Shredding George's back issues of *Bachelor* magazine was a

Very Bad Thing. Losing George's girlfriend's cat was the Worst Thing Ever. He'd be lucky if he ever saw another walkie in his life.

"Inspiring, wasn't it?" John bent down to ruffle Pie's ears.

"Sure was." George put an arm around Nadya's shoulders and gave her a squeeze. "In fact, it made me think I missed my calling. Maybe when we get back to Moscow, I'll take up an instrument. Like the cello. Or the tuba!"

"Maybe I'll get Johanna to ask for a transfer," Beatrix grunted.

Nadya laughed gently. "Or you could start with a simple instrument. Like the guitar."

Nadya was a saint. If JR hadn't been paralyzed with guilt, he would have gone to lie belly up at her feet.

"Great idea!" George picked up an imaginary guitar and began to strum. "I always thought I'd make a great rock star."

Nadya laughed.

"Maybe they won't notice," Robert whispered. "Maybe if we all just keep looking innocent, no one will figure out that—"

"I'm going to find Kisa." Nadya turned and headed for the bedroom.

"Oh no." JR covered his snout with his paws.

"I'll distract her!" Robert sprang into action. He ran a quick lap around the living room, barking all the way, then zipped over to Nadya and blocked her path to the bedroom.

"Robert!" she cried.

"Robert! Stop that!" John marched over and pulled Robert away. "I'm sorry, Nadya. He must be tired of being cooped up. I'll take him outside." Robert tried to wiggle free, but John held fast. Nadya stepped around them and into the bedroom.

"Sorry, J," Robert called as John dragged him toward the door. "I tried!"

"That's okay," JR replied, settling his head on his paws. This was it, then. It was only a matter of seconds before—

"Kisa?" Nadya called from the bedroom. "Kisa!"

He held his breath.

"Stay strong," Beatrix told him. "She'll be upset at first, but it's for the best. That cat was nothing but trouble."

"Right." JR nodded. He knew that. And he was glad to have Kisa out of his fur. He'd been dreaming about it since the moment she invaded his life.

What he didn't want, however, was Nadya upset. He hoped Beatrix was wrong.

"Kisa?" Nadya walked back into the living room, hands on her hips. "Where is she?"

"Not in here," George called from the kitchen.

"Not here either," John said from the front closet, where he was retrieving his walking shoes.

"Then where ...?" Nadya wandered back to the bedroom. "*Kisa?*"

JR wished he were a teacup Shih Tzu, small enough to hide in the flannel folds of the bed. Then he cursed himself, for teacup Shih Tzus were the most ridiculous creatures on earth.

Moments later, Nadya returned, face pale. "She's ... gone!"

"Nah." George emerged from the kitchen, munching on an apple. "She can't be gone. She has to be around somewhere."

"Well, help me search!" Nadya gave him an exasperated look and ran past him into the kitchen. "Kisa!"

"Okay, okay." George put down his apple. "Here kitty, kitty, kitty!" He lifted the couch cushions to look underneath.

"I can't watch this," JR groaned, closing his eyes. The happiness they'd brought home from the concert had completely disappeared. Now the apartment's air was thick with panic and irritation. He tried to take deep breaths.

"Easy, buddy," said Robert. "It'll be okay."

Five minutes later, Nadya and George met back in the living room and agreed, in unison, "She's gone."

Nadya burst into tears.

Tears.

JR hadn't expected tears.

He and George lunged for her at once, George wrapping her in a hug and JR pressing up against her legs. He couldn't believe it. He'd made Nadya cry! Him! Not George the phobic, but JR the terrier. The one who made everything right!

"She must have escaped through the bathroom window!" Nadya sobbed. "But ... but why?"

"Nadya, Kisa was a stray," George said soothingly. "Maybe she just wanted her freedom again."

Yes. Good, George. JR patted his shoe. More of that.

"But I was so good to her." Nadya sniffed. "Why wouldn't she want to stay?"

"You can't take it personally." George rubbed her back.

"Of course I'm taking it personally!" Nadya cried. "She was my cat! How would you feel if JR hopped out a window and ran away?"

JR flinched. This was getting a little too close to home.

"Well, that's silly," said George. "JR wouldn't do that. Would you, buddy?" He glanced down.

JR looked away.

"That's not the point," Nadya said quietly, and she pushed both George and JR away. Before either of them could stop her, she hurried to the bedroom, shutting the door.

Shutting them out.

John took Robert and Pie. "We'll search the sur-rounding streets," he told George. "Don't worry. We'll find that cat."

"I hope so," said George, snapping JR's leash onto his collar.

"We will," John assured him. "Robert and Pie's mother was a search and rescue dog, you know."

"She once found a contact lens in a blue shag carpet," Robert added.

"She was a legend." Pie sighed.

"I'll stay here." Beatrix planted herself by the bedroom door. "Someone has to keep an eye on that one." She jerked her head toward the door, which hadn't opened since Nadya disappeared inside.

"JR and I will search the rest of Josefov." George gave JR a pat on the head and stood up. "And if we can't find her, we'll keep going."

JR nodded, hoping George had remembered to pack some snacks.

The search party bade Beatrix goodbye, then went outside and split up.

JR and George headed first to the courtyard, just in case Kisa was hiding nearby. But there was no sign of her in the grass or trees. Her two stray friends were there, though. They sat on the fence, heads bent together.

"Hey," JR called up at them. "Have you—"

But before he could ask, they leaped off the fence and scampered away.

He sighed, then followed George back out of the courtyard and onto the street.

It was now late afternoon, but still sunny and warm. JR and George trotted up and down the streets of Josefov, past shoppers overloaded with bags, buskers playing violins, and children peering into *cukrárnas*, leaving fingerprints on the windows. The streets teemed with taxis and tourists and, of course, lots of dogs. But there was no sign of a fluffy grey cat with a twitchy tail and big blue eyes.

George called her name a few times, receiving puzzled looks from passersby.

"Lost cat," he explained, but they only shrugged and walked on. "Guess they don't understand English," George said.

But JR wasn't so sure. Maybe the dog-loving Czechs just couldn't imagine why anyone would scour the city for a cat. He couldn't help but wonder himself.

Of course, he didn't want Nadya upset—his stomach still ached at the memory of her tears. But neither did he want Kisa, or any cat, back in his life. Of that he was equally certain.

What was more important, then? Nadya's happiness or his?

He pondered it as they headed for the Vltava, where they found more tourists mulling over maps, more children playing tag on the grass, and more dogs lolling in the sun.

But still, no sign of Kisa.

George sighed. "I guess we just keep walking, boy," he said. "What else can we do?"

JR was fine with that. It felt good to be out and moving his legs. It helped calm the clamour in his head, and he could tell it was making George feel better, too.

They walked and walked, following the river, crossing bridge after bridge, until eventually they came upon a courtyard surrounded by low, cream-coloured buildings.

George stopped and stared at some humans queuing outside. "This is the Kafka Museum," he said. "Boy, it is *weird* in there." He shuddered, then sighed. "But I guess I shouldn't have made such a big deal about it. It's just a museum, after all."

He stared for a moment longer, then gave JR's leash a tug and walked on.

Now the sun was sinking toward the west, and JR's stomach was rumbling. Beatrix and the shepherds were probably having dinner back at home. He considered leading George back, but decided against it. Despite everything, it was actually kind of nice—just the two of them, strolling aimlessly. It was like old times.

George stopped near a bench overlooking the river and a stone church on the opposite bank. He sat down. "Hungry, boy? he asked, rummaging in his coat pocket. He pulled out a custard tart and broke off a piece for JR, who gulped it down without chewing.

They sat there for a while, George on the bench, munching his tart and JR at his feet. The air began to cool as the smell of wet earth drifted off the river.

Maybe ... maybe it wouldn't be so bad, JR mused, if things didn't work out, and it was just him and George again—two bachelors exploring the world. It was a quiet life, sometimes a little lonely, but it wasn't awful. Maybe if they had to leave Moscow, they could move to Prague.

Across the river, church bells began to chime, and a man in a tuxedo stepped out the door, holding the hand of a woman in a long white dress. A few dozen humans filed out after them, smiling and laughing. They all hurried over to the river's edge and began to pose for photos.

Suddenly, George moaned, keeling over and resting his head in his hands. JR looked up, alarmed. Was he sick? Had the tart disagreed with his weak stomach? He leaped up on the bench and nosed his human's neck.

George moaned again, peeking through his fingers at the scene across the river. For a few minutes, he didn't say anything, and JR held his breath. Just how long had that tart been in George's pocket, anyway?

"I can't be happy unless she is, boy," George said into his hands.

JR started and sat back down.

The problem wasn't a bad tart. It was George.

Or rather, it was love.

A bad tart would have been easier to deal with.

George lowered his hands and looked at JR. "You know what I'm saying, boy?"

JR did know. And George had just answered his question.

Nadya's happiness was most important.

They sat there a while longer, until the sun set and the wedding party moved on to their next celebration.

Then they headed home in the dusk, catless.

13

Opening Day

The next morning, Nadya emerged from the bedroom looking like she'd barely slept. Her eyelids drooped and her blouse was buttoned incorrectly.

"Oh good, you're up!" George cried, looking up from his plate of scrambled eggs, which he'd been scrambling into smaller and smaller pieces rather than eating. "Can I get you some breakfast?"

"We've got eggs!" John waved a spatula at her as he cooked some more on the stove.

"I'll make you some toast!" George lunged for the toaster. "It's my specialty."

"No thank you," said Nadya. "I'm not hungry."

George bit his lip. "But you didn't eat anything last night either," he said.

Nadya shrugged, pouring herself a cup of black coffee. "I just don't feel like eating." She didn't sound angry, just ... deflated. "I think I'll take this back to bed," she said, and returned to the bedroom.

George and John looked at each other and sighed. George went back to further scrambling his eggs.

Over by the fireplace, JR's heart was breaking.

"Hey, J," said Robert. "You gonna eat that?" He nodded at JR's dish of kibble, still untouched.

JR couldn't even think about food. "Uh-uh." He rested his head on his paws.

"Well, no sense in it going to waste, right?" Robert made a move for the dish.

"Don't you dare." Beatrix's paw shot out to stop him. "You had your breakfast, and JR needs to eat." She gave JR a stony look. "You *do*."

JR shook his head. "I can't. I don't feel well." In fact, he'd never felt worse, not even the time he'd eaten George's sunglasses and a piece had gotten lodged in his stomach. The pain of intestinal surgery had nothing on the pain that came with making George's girlfriend very, very sad.

He was officially a Bad Terrier.

"Breakfast," Beatrix informed him, "is the most important meal of the day. Especially when you have an important job to do. You can't expect to be a good director if you haven't eaten breakfast."

"She's right, JR," Pie whispered, sidling over and lying down next to him. "Come on, eat your kibble. If you can't do it for yourself, do it for the circus. Today is Opening Day!"

JR groaned. The circus was the last thing he wanted to think about. How could he possibly go direct a show now? If being a good director was indeed like being a good terrier, well, then he wasn't cut out for the job.

"That's it." George stood up suddenly, pushing away his now thoroughly scrambled eggs. "We're doing it."

JR raised his head.

John looked up from his toast. "Doing what?"

George took a deep breath. He paused for a moment, as if unsure whether he was actually capable of the drastic action he was about to take.

"We're going to the bone museum!" George announced.

JR's belly filled with warmth. George was a good human.

"Yes," George said, as if to convince himself. "We're doing it." And he marched into the bedroom.

Half an hour later, they were ready to go.

"Well, this'll be interesting," John said, a little too brightly. "We'll make a day of it."

George nodded. "We'll go for lunch, maybe some dumplings ... We probably won't be back till the evening." He turned to JR. "Think you can hold it, boy?"

JR returned a reassuring look. If George could visit a museum of human remains, he could hold it till they returned.

"Are you excited?" George helped Nadya into her jacket. "There'll be bones! Lots of 'em!"

Nadya tried to smile, but JR could sense her sadness as clearly as he could sense Pie's anxiety at having to hold it all day. She nodded. "Of course."

JR's heart broke into a few more pieces, like George's over-scrambled eggs. Was this it? he wondered. Was the damage now done? Would Nadya never be happy again? He whimpered.

"Easy, J," Robert said under his breath.

"Keep it together," Beatrix murmured.

He took a deep breath and tried his best to keep it together.

The humans bade the dogs goodbye and left. The door closed firmly behind them.

"Well?" Beatrix turned to the others. "Shall we?"

Robert hopped to his feet. "We couldn't have planned this better ourselves. Old Niko's too superstitious to let our humans near the circus, so they get right outta town." He licked his lips. "Too perfect."

"I'm so excited!" Pie whispered, trembling all over. "It'll be my first circus performance!"

"Come on, J." Robert nosed him firmly. "Forget about your humans and focus on the circus. It's Opening Day, and it's gonna be great."

JR looked at the front door. How could he possibly forget about his humans?

"It's out of your paws now," said Beatrix.

As awful as that felt, he had to admit she was right. There was nothing he could do.

"Okay." He took a deep breath, trying to focus on the circus. "We're doing it."

"There it is!" Pie squealed when the big top came into view. "Have you ever seen anything more beautiful? Is there anywhere else you'd rather be right now?"

Even JR, who would much rather have been curled up on the couch with George and Nadya, had to admit the red-and-white-striped tents were an impressive sight. According to his stomach, it was about lunchtime, which meant the show would open in just two hours.

Already, the circus grounds were abuzz with the squeals of children and the laughter of their parents. JR's heart began to beat faster. All these people had come to see Circus Sergei. Now it was up to him and the animals to put on a show they'd never forget.

"Wait." Robert stopped suddenly, eyes wide. "What are *those*?"

Pie gasped and froze.

JR did a double take. Next to the ticket booth, four humans in black satin robes were marching around, waving at the children swarming around their feet.

Except these weren't just any humans. These humans were about twelve feet tall. Their heads nearly grazed the telephone wires overhead.

"Giants!" Pie shrieked. "Like on that movie we watched with John! Remember, Robert?"

"They've come to take over the earth!" Robert whispered.

"Y-you think?" JR gasped.

Beatrix rolled her eyes. "Those are stilt walkers," she said.

"Call 'em what you want," said Robert. "But I'm getting the heck outta here." He turned to run away, but Beatrix caught him by the scruff.

"They're *circus performers*, bonehead!" she growled. "They're standing on stilts to make themselves taller."

"What?" Robert took another look. "Really?"

"Wow." JR had never seen anything like them. "I didn't know Circus Sergei had stilt walkers."

"We must not have seen all the performers yet," said Beatrix. "Come on." She led them closer, sticking to the trees so they didn't draw too much attention. Not that it mattered much, since everyone was watching the stilt walkers in their long, black robes, each one decorated with a black half moon.

"Looks like they're giving out tickets," JR observed, watching one of the performers lean down and hand a piece of paper to a delighted child, who shrieked and waved it around. A couple stepped up and accepted two tickets, followed by a family of four.

"Maybe sales haven't been so good," Robert suggested.

"Maybe," said JR. But something about the scene felt wrong. He just couldn't put his paw on what. He stared hard at the stilt walkers, until suddenly, it dawned on him.

"Hey, wait a second ..."

Just then, Sergei himself came marching out, shouting something in Russian.

"Huh," said Robert. "What's up with him?"

As they watched, Sergei marched right up to one of the stilt walkers. Then he wound up and booted the performer in his wooden shin. The stilt walker reeled, flailing his arms.

"What's he doing?" Pie cried. "That's his own performer! He's sabotaging his own act!"

"Wait!" JR jumped in front of him before Pie could go barrelling off to save his kind. "They're not from Circus Sergei!"

"What?" Robert looked at him.

JR shook his head. "Look at their robes. See the half moons?"

Beatrix squinted. "Yes. So what?"

"There was a half moon like that on the jacket Masha brought to the barn the other night. The stilt walkers"—he gulped—"are from Circus Magnificus."

Robert's eyes grew wide. "Circus Magnificus is handing out free tickets?"

"Right in front of Circus Sergei?" Pie added. "Just hours before it starts?"

"Why those nasty—" Beatrix began.

"Come on." JR turned and led them past Sergei, who was now chasing one of the stilt walkers around in circles. They made a break for the barn and zipped inside, only to find their friends in complete despair.

"Did you see?" cried the chimp. "Circus Magnificus is stealing our audience!"

"We've barely sold any of our own tickets," moaned the elephant.

"That's it." The goose threw up his wings. "We're done like dinner. Just call me foie gras!"

"Wait!" JR yelled. "Everyone, just … just calm down. We'll get through this!"

A half-dozen snouts, beaks, and trunks turned to him. "How?" they asked.

"Well …" He hadn't quite figured that out yet. "Let's think." He sat down on the dirt floor, and they gathered around him. "Come on, guys," he said. "What do we need?"

"We need to get rid of those intruders," the chimp declared.

"I could chase them away," the tiger offered.

JR shook his head, imagining a tiger loose in the middle of Prague. "Too risky."

"We need to sabotage Circus Magnificus!" crowed one of the parrots.

"It's too late for that," said Beatrix. "What we need is to get people past those stilt walkers and into our big top. Lots of them, and right away."

"We need an act to draw them in!" The chimp jabbed a finger in the air.

"Right!" JR nodded. "Now we're thinking!"

"I could recite my new poem," Pie offered.

"Maybe something with more action," said the chimp. He turned to the kangaroo. "You could do your routine."

But she shook her head. "My trampoline's in the big top."

JR chewed on his lip, racking his brain. What they needed was a showstopper—a new act that would make the humans stop and stare. And preferably an animal act, since convincing a human to perform would be challenging, if not impossible.

They needed—

"Kisa." The word escaped JR's mouth before he even knew it.

The dogs turned to him, eyes wide, and his own eyes widened as he realized it was true.

They needed Kisa.

14

An Apology

"The *cat*?" Beatrix couldn't believe it.

JR nodded. "The cat."

"Like, the one you just got rid of?" Robert cocked his head to one side. Pie cocked his head to the other.

"Uh-huh." JR nodded faster. "She could show up undetected, without causing a commotion. And she could do her crazy trick!"

His friends looked at him like he had a bad case of rabies.

"She can walk the tightrope!" JR went on. "You guys didn't see it, but I did. *Kisa* is the showstopper we need."

"But ... but ... she's a cat!" Beatrix cried.

JR nodded. "I know."

"And last I checked, you didn't *like* cats," Robert pointed out.

"I don't!" JR insisted. "That's not the point! The circus needs Kisa so the show can go on!"

Beatrix and Robert exchanged another glance, still unconvinced. The other animals stayed quiet, watching them.

"I think JR's right," the kangaroo spoke up. "The circus hasn't had a tightrope walker since Masha's mother left. This cat might be just what we need to draw in a crowd."

"Yes!" JR cried. "Exactly!"

"But the show starts in a few hours," Robert pointed out. "We don't know where she is."

"Then we have to find her!" said JR.

"Right!" cried Pie. He turned to JR. "And just how are we going to do that?"

JR sat down to think again. The other dogs sat as well, and the animals followed suit.

"What if we asked some cats where she is?" suggested Robert. "It'd involve talking to cats, but it might work."

"Good idea," said JR. "What about her friends back at the apartment?"

"The ones we chased the other day?" asked Robert.

"Yeah."

Robert chuckled. "We could try."

"Now wait just a doggone minute!" Beatrix cut in. "Let me get this straight. We're going back to the apartment to find the stray cats we chased the other day."

"Right." JR nodded.

"And then we're going to *talk* to them."

"Yup," said Robert.

"But ... they're *cats*!"

"Look, you don't have to come," JR told her. "And neither do you," he added to Robert and Pie. "But I ... I know this is the right thing to do." He stood up. "So I'm going, right now. There's no time to lose."

Robert leaped to his feet. "I'm in."

"You're not going without me." Pie glued himself to his brother's side.

They turned to Beatrix, who tossed her hair and looked away.

JR nodded to the shepherds, and they turned to leave.

"Fine," Beatrix said. "I'll come. But only because I'm the one with the powers of persuasion."

JR chose not to answer that, turning instead to the animals. "We'll be right back," he promised. "We're going to get you a showstopper!"

The dogs sprinted past the stilt walkers and the crowd at the front gates, then zipped back down the hill to the Vltava. Dodging tourists and children and ignoring the questioning looks of other dogs, they ran along the riverbank, crossed a bridge, then sprinted down the streets of Josefov.

By the time they reached the apartment, they were all panting and sweaty. They headed around back to the courtyard and stopped to catch their breath.

"I don't see them," Pie said, looking around.

"What if they're not here?" Robert asked.

JR tuned into his Terrier Senses. "Oh, they're here," he said. "I can't see them, but I can tell. And they're watching us." He shivered.

"Hey there, cats!" Robert called out. "We're looking for your friend! You know, the fluffy grey flea—I mean, uh, feline."

But there was no answer. Not even a meow.

"This is useless," Beatrix huffed.

"No, it's not," JR said. They were listening—he just knew it. And what's more, he knew they wanted something.

He took a deep breath.

"Excuse me," he called. "Um, we hate to bother you, since we know you're ... busy."

Beatrix snorted.

"Shh." Robert nudged her.

"But we're looking for your friend," JR continued. "We need her ..." He glanced at his friends. "Help."

"We do not—" Beatrix began, but Robert shushed her again.

"We do," JR insisted to the courtyard.

"What do you want?" someone demanded, and they all whirled around to see two cats—a tabby and a black and white—slinking their way. Neither looked pleased.

"Oh, um, hi." He took a few steps back. The cats continued to creep forward, tails waving in tandem.

"You're disturbing us," said the tabby.

"You should go back inside where you belong," said the black and white.

"On-leash," added the tabby.

Pie whimpered and hid behind Robert.

"This is important." JR squared his shoulders. "We're trying to find your friend. My humans took her in the day after we ... met you."

"We know," said the black and white.

"She was never cut out for street life." The tabby sniffed.

"Right." JR nodded. "Anyway, she ..." He swallowed, wondering how well cats could detect lies. "She got away."

The tabby stopped and gave him a long once-over, from nose to tail and back again. "What's your name?"

"JR," he said. "And this is Robert, Pie, and Beatrix."

"G'day," said Robert.

"Pleased to meet you!" squeaked Pie, peeking out from behind his brother.

Beatrix said nothing.

"I am Magda," said the tabby.

"Lubos," offered the black and white.

"Okay." JR felt slightly better now that they were on first-name terms. "So ... any idea where Kisa went?"

"Her name," Magda informed him, "is Drahomira."

"Oh." JR started. It had never occurred to him that Kisa already had a name.

"Draho-what now?" asked Robert.

Magda glared at him.

"Okay," JR said quickly. "Drahomira, then."

"And as a matter of fact"—Magda turned her nose skyward—"we do know where she is."

"Really?" JR's tail pricked up.

"But we're not telling you."

"Oh." His tail sagged.

"I told you," Beatrix murmured. "Sneaky little fleaballs."

JR turned back to Lubos and Magda. "What's it going to take?"

For a moment, they said nothing—only waved their tails back and forth, back and forth.

"Hmm." Lubos made a show of contemplating the question. "How about an apology?"

That was what JR had been afraid of.

"That's it. I'm out." Beatrix turned. "Keeshonds don't apologize to cats."

"Wait!" JR raced around and planted himself in front of her. "We have to."

"We most certainly do not!" She glowered at him.

"Okay, we don't *have* to," he admitted. "And okay, it won't be fun. But it'll be worth it. Come on."

She looked away.

"Think about it, Bea," said Robert. "If we find Draho ... what's-her-fur and bring her back, we'll get a big crowd. That means people in the seats when it's your turn to shine."

Beatrix thought it over for a minute.

"Just imagine a sold-out show," JR added. "All eyes on you."

Finally, she grunted her assent. "But this goes against everything I believe in."

"I know." Relieved, JR turned back to the cats. He took a deep breath and readied himself to do something he'd never thought he'd do. "We're sorry," he told them.

"For?" Magda sharpened her claws on a cobble-stone. The sound made JR's neck hair stand on end.

"Chasing you. Barking at you. Calling you fleaballs. You know."

"You're all sorry?" Lubos asked. "All of you?" His green eyes landed on Beatrix.

The dogs all nodded.

"Hey!" Magda shouted. "Fluffy's crossing her legs!"

"I am not!" Beatrix said, uncrossing her legs. "And at least I've got hair, you mangy minx," she added under her breath.

For a moment, they all regarded each other carefully. Finally, the cats nodded.

"Well, that was fun," said Magda, inspecting her claws. She rose and stretched, then turned to go.

"Wait!" JR cried. "Where's Kisa? I mean Drahomira."

"Oh." Magda turned back. "She's not here."

"What?" JR cried. "Where is she then?"

"She left," said Lubos. "She went to ..." He looked to Magda for approval. "Stag Moat."

JR's toes curled. "Where?" he asked, hoping he'd heard wrong.

"Stag Moat," said Pie. "You remember, don't you? The big, dark forest with all the—"

"I know!" JR snapped. He turned back to the cats. "Why'd she go there?"

"She's been through a lot," said Magda. "She needed some me-time."

"Some what?" JR cocked his head.

"What's that?" asked Robert.

"It sounds frightening," whispered Pie.

Magda sighed. "Forget it. You dogs wouldn't understand me-time. You can't even spend an entire day alone without eating your human's purse."

"That's not true," JR protested.

"Actually, it is," said Pie. "But who would want to spend an entire day alone?"

Magda rolled her eyes.

"Okay, fine," JR said. "We need to go to Stag Moat. Now. We have to be back at Letna Park in an hour."

"Good luck with that," said Magda. "It's too far, even if you run."

"We'll try it anyway," JR insisted. "We're fast."

"You'll never make it," Magda said. "There's no way. Not unless you're somehow able to take the metro," she added dryly.

"Well, maybe—"JR stopped as her words sank in. "Wait. There's a metro?"

"Of course there's a metro." She rolled her eyes.

"Well, why didn't you say so?" he cried, leaping up into the air. "Where's the nearest station?"

15

The Cats of Stag Moat

At Lubos's instruction, they hightailed it to Staromětská metro station, the closest to their apartment. Just as he'd said, it was clearly marked with a street sign—a big red M with an arrow pointing down the staircase to the underground trains.

"Guys," Robert panted as they all stopped on the busy street, ignoring the stares of passersby. "I've been thinking. This might not be such a good idea."

JR whirled to face him. "What do you mean? We're almost there!"

Robert gestured for them all to put their snouts together. "Just hear me out. Praha might be a city of dog lovers, but it's not Moscow, and the humans aren't used to seeing even one dog on the metro, let alone four."

Beatrix nodded. "Robert's right. It's too dangerous."

JR couldn't believe it. "Are you kidding? We can't turn back now!"

Beatrix shook her head. "I don't mean we should turn back. At least, not all of us."

"But we ... oh." JR fell silent as he realized what they meant. Four dogs on the Prague metro would be too many. But one dog ... especially one average-sized Jack Russell terrier ...

"Okay. I'll go on alone," he said, trying not to think about what this would entail.

"Are you sure?" Pie's eyes were enormous. "Won't you be scared?"

"Uh-uh." JR shook his head, hoping they couldn't see his hind legs trembling. "I'm sure it's just like the metro in Moscow. Which I've taken dozens of times," he added, more to convince himself than his friends.

"If anyone can do this, it's you, buddy." Robert gave him an encouraging head-butt.

"Do you remember Lubos's instructions?" asked Beatrix.

JR nodded. "Take the green line toward Dejvická. Get off at Malostranská. On the way back, I'll have to take the tram, and get off at Čechův Most."

"Yes." Pie nodded. "I have no idea what any of that means."

"That's why JR's going, and not us," Robert told him.

"Enough chit-chat," said Beatrix. "We'll meet you at the circus grounds in an hour."

"Right." JR set off down the staircase before the sensible voice in his brain could object to him travelling by metro in a foreign country to find a stray cat in a forest and bring her back to save a circus.

"You can do this," he told himself. The strays in Moscow had taught him well. Plus, Lubos had given him good, detailed instructions.

It was the first time in his life he was grateful for a cat.

The challenge would be not drawing attention. Fortunately, humans in the metro were usually too focused on reaching their destinations to notice much else.

He chose a man in a smart grey suit and stuck close to him, pretending the man was his human. Absorbed in a conversation on his phone, the man didn't even notice. He stopped to feed his ticket into a machine and continued on. JR followed, unseen.

So far, so good.

He followed the man down a dark hallway, trying to keep tabs on his trousers among a swarm of jeans and skirts and shorts. He was so focused on following the trousers, in fact, that he didn't notice the black leather boots beside him until it was too late.

The boots stopped beside the trousers, and JR looked up to see a mustachioed policeman in a blue shirt and hat, looking unimpressed. He gestured at JR, and the man looked down and did a double take.

JR blinked back innocently.

The policeman said something that JR guessed meant, "What do you think you're doing with a dog in the metro?" and the man answered with what probably meant, "I've never seen this dog in my life!" An argument ensued.

JR took that as his cue to slip away into the swarm of jeans and skirts and shorts. A few moments later, he heard a scuffle behind him, but he held his breath and kept going, trying to think himself very small. Like a teacup Shih Tzu. But with a brain.

Once he was fairly certain he'd lost the policeman, he chose a woman pushing a baby stroller and pressed himself against the stroller's side. The woman was too busy cooing at the baby to notice. In fact, she only looked up once, to check the sign overhead directing them toward the green line.

Only then did JR allow himself to breathe. Everything was back under control. Now he just had to make sure he caught the train going in the right direction, toward Dejvická. If he took the one headed in the wrong direction, he'd lose precious time. He tried his best to tune out all the rumbles and chatter around him so he could hear the human voice announcing the next train.

Moments later, the ground under his paws began to tremble and shake, and an enormous grey train thundered up beside them and screeched to a halt.

"Dejvická," said the announcer, and JR breathed a sigh of relief. He waited until the passengers had surged off the train, then hopped on board before the doors could slam shut. Then he called to mind the Moscow dogs' Number One Rule of taking the metro: always look like you know what you're doing, even when you don't.

Especially when you don't.

He squared his shoulders, pointed his snout toward the ceiling, and strutted down the aisle between the seats, channelling Beatrix in her kibble commercial. He chose a spot next to an old man in loafers, and for a moment considered hopping up on the bench beside him. But he decided that might be pushing it, and instead settled at the man's feet.

The woman opposite them smiled at him, then said something to the man—probably asking if JR belonged to him. The man shook his head, and the woman seemed surprised. They both looked down at JR, then at the people around them.

"Humans," JR muttered. Why did they have to be so nosy?

Fortunately, the train reached Malostranská station before any of them could solve the mystery of the off-leash terrier. The doors swung open, and JR stood, nodded good day to them all, then marched off the train and onto the platform.

Laughter rang out behind him, but he didn't pause to acknowledge it, or even congratulate himself on what he'd done. Now it was on to Stag Moat.

By the time he reached the forest, JR's throat was parched and his heart was hammering. He paused on a stone bridge over the creek to catch his breath and summon his courage for what came next. There was nothing he wanted to do less than venture into the woods. But he forced himself to put one paw in front of the other and continue across the bridge.

The moment he left the paved path, the sun slipped behind the trees. Some crows squawked overhead. JR chewed his lip, trying to ignore all the Terrier Senses telling him to stop. Every hair on his body was standing on end.

You can do this, he told himself. If George can face his phobia, you can, too.

He pictured George marching off to the bone museum, summer scarf flapping in the breeze, and tried to channel his human's resolve.

It was the first time he'd ever tried to channel George.

There were cats everywhere, all around him. And they knew he was there. They were watching him.

"Hello!" he called up to the branches. "I'm, um, looking for Kisa. I mean Drahomira. Can someone help me?"

But there was no answer. The woods were eerily still.

"Come on, please?" he added. "I know you can hear me!"

Still no answer. Not even a meow.

Suddenly, something burst out of a shrub behind him, and JR yelped, leaping a foot off the ground. A black cat streaked by him and darted into another bush. Her laughter trailed behind.

"Scaredy-dog!" a voice sang out. More laughter followed.

JR turned hot with shame. This was a terrible idea. What had he been thinking?

He turned to leave.

But he'd only taken a few steps before the image of his human popped back into his mind. If George could do it ...

He closed his eyes, found a few more drops of courage, and turned back around.

"What do you want?"

He opened his eyes to see Kisa sitting on a patch of moss, her fluffy grey tail waving back and forth.

"Kisa!" he cried, bounding over to her. She jumped backward.

He stopped. "Sorry. I was just ... happy to see you."

"Stay where you are," she told him.

"Okay." He sat down. "Look. I know this is weird. But I need your help. No, just hear me out," he rushed on before she could answer. "You know those tricks you do? Where you balance like a tight-rope walker? Well, I'm hoping you can come with me and do them for some humans. Like, now-ish."

She looked at him like he'd grown another set of ears.

"It's not for me," he went on. "It's for Circus Sergei. Or rather, for Nadya's family."

She only stared at him, eyes still narrowed.

"And maybe it'll be a good chance for you to show off your skills?" he added, getting desperate now. "Because they're really impressive. I know I never said that before, but they are." He swallowed hard. "What do you think?"

For a moment, she stayed silent. Finally, she said, "I think you've got a lot of nerve."

His tail drooped. She was right.

"Look, I'm sorry," he said. "For being a jerk. For chasing you away." He looked down at his paws. "I ... I didn't know Nadya liked cats. It was a bit of a shock. And, well, I didn't want to share my life with one."

Kisa stayed silent for several minutes more. Then, just as JR was beginning to lose all hope, she said, "You weren't just being a jerk to me, you know. You were being a jerk to Nadya."

"What?" JR started. "That's not true!"

Kisa nodded. "Is too. Nadya just wanted a pet, and you were trying to stop her from having what would make her happy."

"But Nadya has a pet!" he protested. "She has me!"

Kisa sighed. "You don't get it, do you? You're George's, first and foremost. You two are inseparable—he's devoted to you. Any idiot can see that."

JR swallowed. "Really?"

"Obviously," said Kisa. "And Nadya was never allowed to have a pet growing up. This was her chance."

JR chewed on his lip. Nadya *had* said that a few times lately. "Okay," he admitted. "You might be right. I messed up. And I'm sorry."

Kisa stayed quiet for a moment. "Do you mean it?" she said finally. "Are you really sorry?"

JR nodded. "Yeah."

"Because Nadya's upset?"

"Well, yeah. I mean, no. That is ..."

Kisa waited.

"No," he said finally. "I'm sorry I made you upset."

"Really?"

He sighed. "You're going to make me say it *again*?"

She smoothed her whiskers. "Okay. Apology accepted. But we're not friends."

"That's okay," JR said quickly. "We don't have to be friends."

Kisa nodded. "Good."

"Okay."

They fell silent, avoiding each other's eyes.

"So what's this about a circus?" asked Kisa.

JR drew a breath and filled her in as quickly as possible.

She thought about it for a moment, then shook her head. "I don't know."

"Please?" JR begged. "Just once? If you hate it, you'll never have to do it again. But I think you'll like it." At least, he hoped so.

Kisa looked up at the treetops, then back down at JR. "All right, fine," she said. "But just this once. And for Nadya."

JR leaped up in the air. "Yeah! Thanks Kisa!" Then he stopped. "I mean, Drahomira."

She twitched her tail. "Let's stick with Kisa. It's not a bad nickname."

JR sighed with relief. "Great. Perfect. But now we've got to hurry. The show will be starting in less than an hour. And we've got to get to Letna Park."

"Letna Park!" she cried. "But that's so far! How are we going to get there?"

JR turned to face her. "How about I tell you on the way?"

16
Tram Travel

"There it is." JR pointed with his snout toward the approaching red-and-white tram. It was like an above-ground metro car, attached to rail lines on the street and cables overhead.

"This is crazy." Kisa's blue eyes were wider than he'd ever seen them. "Cats don't take transit!"

"Just don't think about it," JR advised her, heading for a crowd of waiting humans. "Follow me."

He darted toward a woman in a big, flowy skirt, then ushered Kisa into the folds. When the woman stepped off the sidewalk to meet the approaching tram, they moved with her, huddling close to her ankles while she climbed the stairs.

"This is so wrong," Kisa whispered.

"It's only one stop," JR told her, peeking out of the skirt. "We'll be there in no time. Come on." He headed back out.

"I can't believe I agreed to do this for a human!" she cried, scrambling after him.

"It's not just any human!" JR reminded her, trotting down the aisle between the seats. "It's Nadya. She's special."

"She'd better be a cat food dispenser in disguise," Kisa grumbled.

JR chose a spot near the rear doors and motioned for Kisa to join him.

"Yikes!" she yelled as the tram lurched forward.

"Just sit down," he said, "and try to look like you know what you're doing. That way, no one will question you."

"Fat chance," she said, and sure enough, a man standing nearby pointed at them and exclaimed something. A woman burst into laughter, and her son took out his camera and snapped a photo of JR and Kisa. Soon all the passengers were chuckling.

"I hate this," Kisa said through clenched teeth.

"Just act natural," JR whispered back, mugging for another photo. "It's all good as long as they're entertained." He tapped his paw on the floor, counting down the seconds till they could disembark.

The tram slowed, then lurched to a halt. The doors banged open.

"Finally!" Kisa leaped to her feet.

"Wait," said JR. Something felt wrong. "I don't know if this is the stop ..." He craned his neck to see what was going on.

Kisa groaned as another man crouched to take their picture. She stuck out her tongue.

A familiar smell wafted over, and JR took a big sniff, trying to place it. It was the smell of rubber and leather, kind of like George's winter boots. Except different somehow ...

He turned toward the smell and saw two big black boots.

Two big black boots on the feet of a mustachioed policeman.

"Oh no!" JR gasped. The policeman was checking passengers' tickets, making sure they'd all paid their fare. "Quick! This way!" He pushed Kisa in the opposite direction, toward a man in jeans and sneakers. They zipped behind the man's legs, but weren't fast enough. The man shouted and raised a sneaker in Kisa's direction.

"Look out!" JR pushed her out of the sneaker's way. It missed her, but JR's shove caught her off guard, and she went sliding across the floor.

Right into the policeman's boot.

"No!" JR watched in horror as the policeman looked down to find a fluffy grey cat on his foot. His mouth opened to a shout.

"Run, Kisa!" JR hollered. "Run!"

The policeman leaned over to grab her, but Kisa was too quick. Yowling, she leaped up and shot across the car. A few passengers shrieked as she ricocheted overhead.

"Please stop, please stop," JR begged the tram. "Let us off!"

He was so busy begging that he didn't see the policeman until his hand clamped down on his collar. With a triumphant grunt, the man lifted him up by the scruff of his neck.

JR gasped and squirmed, his legs dangling a good five feet off the floor. The policeman held tight—so tight that JR could barely breathe. He was beginning to see stars. Or maybe it was his life flashing before his eyes. Yes, that was it. There was the farm where he was born, back in Canada. And there was George, picking him out of the litter. But what was that grey thing, headed right for him? And why—

Whump.

The policeman let go of his scruff and the stars disappeared, giving JR a clear view of the grey ball of fur that had just smacked the man in the face. Had he not been plummeting toward the ground, JR would have cheered.

He hit the floor with a *thunk* just as the doors burst open.

"Our stop!" he yelled, bouncing back up.

"Let's get out of here!" Kisa shrieked.

They shot out the door as the policeman began to roar. Neither dog nor cat looked back as they leaped out into the sunshine.

The circus tents had just come into view when Kisa stopped again.

JR drew up beside her. "Hey, don't stop now. We're almost there. And the show's about to start!"

But Kisa shook her head. "I need to say something."

"Now?" JR couldn't believe it.

She glared at him. "Do you realize what you just put me through?"

"Okay, fine." He sighed. "What?"

She paused for a moment, and he shifted from paw to paw, impatient. He could hear the orchestra warming up in the big top.

"Okay," she said finally. "Back at the apartment, when you went full pit bull on me? I was just trying to be your friend."

"But why?" JR wrinkled his nose. "Dogs and cats aren't friends."

"But we could be," said Kisa. "Look, you want to know the reason I'm a stray?"

JR nodded.

"My humans had a pair of Pomeranians, and we didn't get along at all. We fought all the time."

JR couldn't blame her for that. Pomeranians were the worst.

"But my humans preferred dogs," Kisa went on. "So, eventually they moved away and left me behind."

"Oh." JR's stomach lurched. "That's awful, Kisa."

Kisa nodded. "I didn't want that to happen again. I wanted us to get along, since George and Nadya are obviously crazy about you. Anyone can see that."

"Really?" asked JR. "You can tell?"

"Of course!" said Kisa. "So I wanted to be your friend, and help you out."

"Help me?" JR wrinkled his nose. "I don't need help."

"Yes you do," Kisa replied. "You need someone to look out for you."

"What? I do not!"

"You dogs!" She rolled her eyes. "You spend all your time running around trying to please people, trying to keep them happy. And you never take care of yourselves. We cats get it—we know how to put our needs first, then help humans later. We're smart like that."

JR opened his mouth to argue, then paused as her words sank in. He *did* spend an awful lot of time trying to keep George and Nadya happy. But that was his role. That's what a good terrier did.

Wasn't it?

He suddenly remembered the flight attendant's instructions about securing your own mask before helping others. You were useless if you didn't take care of yourself first.

Supposing Kisa was right?

"Well ..." He chewed his lip. "Thanks, then. For ... looking out for me." It felt very strange to be saying that—and to a cat, of all creatures.

But then, maybe Kisa wasn't just any old cat. She had saved him from a policeman, after all.

"Nice work back there," he added. "That was pretty impressive."

"Thanks," she said. "I wish I could have seen his face."

JR chuckled.

"Okay." Kisa straightened. "So what do I do now?"

JR pointed with his nose toward the entrance. "See that wire up there?"

Kisa nodded.

"I need you to get up there and walk it. Right side up, upside down. Put on a show."

"That's it?" she asked.

"That's it."

She smoothed her whiskers. "No problem." And she stood up and trotted off toward the entrance, her fluffy grey tail held high.

Minutes later, a crowd began to gather, staring at the tightrope-walking cat above their heads. Kisa flipped and twirled, tiptoeing from one end to the other and back. The humans oohed and aahed. A few rushed for the ticket booth.

"Yes!" JR cheered. Then he turned and headed for the barn, to ready the performers for the big show.

17

Circus Animalius

The crowd was going wild.

They cheered as the chimp swung harder and faster on the parallel bars. They gasped as he turned a triple flip. They booed when a clown attempted to drag him off.

The clown raced back out of the ring, empty-handed, and joined a huddle of human performers watching, bewildered, as the animals hijacked their show. Several of them had already tried to coax the animals out of the ring, to no avail.

"What are we going to do?" one of the dancers wailed.

The clown threw up his hands. "Not much we can do," he said. "Until someone finds Sergei!"

From the shadows near their feet, JR took in the action, practically bursting with pride.

"What's going on?" Two new humans squeezed their way to the front of the crowd and came to a stop beside JR. He looked up to see Masha and Niko staring, open mouthed, at the chimp on the parallel bars.

"What on earth?" breathed Niko.

"He's ... he's ..." Masha burst into laughter.

JR's ears pricked up as a new idea came to mind. It would involve trying to communicate with Masha and Niko, but they were understanding humans. At least, he hoped so.

He crept out of the shadows toward their feet, then placed a paw on each of their shins.

Masha looked down and gasped.

"JR?" Niko did a double take.

Masha began to laugh again, and crouched to scratch JR's ears. "Do you have something to do with this?" she asked him.

"This is crazy!" Niko ran a hand through his hair. "Where's Sergei?"

"Nowhere to be found," the clown said helplessly.

JR nosed Masha's hand, then pointed his snout toward the ring. She followed his gaze, then nodded, understanding as he had hoped she would.

She rose, dusted off her jeans, and stepped away.

"Wait!" Niko cried, but she was already in the ring, walking toward the parallel bars.

The crowd murmured as the small girl walked over to the chimp, holding out her arms. Grinning, he took one final swing, finishing off with a flip and a double twist, then landing square on his feet in front of Masha.

She grabbed his hand and raised it in the air. "Ladies and gentlemen!" she called to the audience. "Let's hear it for the chimp!"

The cheers were like thunder.

"You were amazing!" JR yelled as the chimp and Masha jogged past him, heading back to the barn. The chimp returned a thumbs-up. "Okay, where's the kangaroo?" JR looked around. "She's up next!"

On cue, the kangaroo bounded out of the shadows, cutting off a troupe of dancers, who shrieked as she bounced past on her way to the trampoline.

The audience roared. JR's hind legs danced a jig.

"This is incredible." Niko kneeled beside JR and put a hand on his head, as if to steady himself. "And you—how did you get here? Do you have something to do with—" Then he shook his head. "No, that's impossible. Right?" he added, raising an eyebrow at JR.

JR returned a steady look.

Soon Masha returned, breathless and flushed.

"Go get the kangaroo!" one of the dancers commanded. "You're the only one the animals will listen to!"

With a grin, Masha jogged into the ring again, returning moments later leading the leaping kangaroo. The crowd's applause was deafening.

"That felt terrific!" the kangaroo cried as she passed.

"You looked terrific!" JR told her. "Great work." Then he turned back to Niko, who was staring after his daughter.

JR held his breath, sending Niko his strongest, most encouraging vibes.

Finally, Niko looked back at JR. "It's a brand-new show tonight, isn't it?" he said. "Time for a change."

Then he took a deep breath, stood, and ran into the ring, where the Chinese Pole awaited.

Niko cleared his throat and shook the newspaper to get everyone's attention.

"What does it say? What does it say?" Masha hopped from one foot to the other.

"Don't keep us hanging!" George added.

JR barked in agreement. This would be his very first review. His knees trembled at the thought.

It was the morning after Opening Day, and they were all gathered in the courtyard behind the apartment building: five humans, four dogs, and one fluffy grey cat.

"Ready?" Niko winked at his daughter.

"Read it!" Masha laughed. "We can't wait!"

Niko cleared his throat again. "The new and improved Circus Sergei is a surprise hit," he read, and everyone cheered. "No longer just a predictable lineup of acrobats and clowns, it shines the spotlight on the circus's animals, letting them show off their natural talents!"

"Hooray!" Masha gave Pie a hug.

"I can't wait to see it this afternoon," said George.

"And it's a good thing Niko got us tickets," added John. "After yesterday's performance, nearly all the shows are sold out."

Niko continued reading. "Highlights included the appearance of a talented young animal handler and a stunning new Chinese Pole routine by Niko the trapeze artist."

Once the applause had subsided, he continued: "This bold and creative new vision is exactly what Circus Sergei needed. When finally reached for a statement, Director Sergei told reporters he'd been planning the new show for some time—that even small traditional circuses like his need to change now and then."

"Really?" John raised an eyebrow. "He was planning it all along?"

"Not a chance," Niko answered. "He was nowhere to be found during the show."

"Was it hard to subdue him?" Beatrix asked Robert.

"He wasn't about to argue with the tiger chasing him into the elephant's stall," Robert said. "Once he realized he couldn't get out, he just sat down and took a nap." He grinned. "I think he needed a break."

"So if Sergei wasn't directing the new show, who was behind it?" asked George.

Niko shrugged. "Maybe the animals."

The dogs drew in a breath.

George laughed. "Now that'd be something!"

"It'd make quite a story," said John.

Masha winked at JR, who let out his breath. Masha and Niko were going to keep his secret. They were excellent humans. The very best.

"Anyway, if Sergei claims this new show was his idea," Niko went on, "he can't very well go back to the old one. So you'll definitely be seeing my Chinese Pole routine this afternoon."

"Trust a human to take credit for someone else's ideas," Beatrix huffed.

But JR himself wasn't upset. "It's okay," he told his friends. "Niko's right—this just means the new show is here to stay. Which is good since we've only got a few more days in town."

"Actually," Niko went on, "when I spoke with Sergei this morning, he was thinking of renaming the show Circus Animalius, to highlight the new stars."

"Perfect." Masha sighed.

"I guess Sergei realized that change isn't so scary after all," John concluded.

"Good for him," said George. "Sometimes you just have to face your fears." He reached over and gave Nadya's hand a squeeze, and she smiled back.

Apparently, the bone museum hadn't been nearly as awful as George himself had feared. "It was actually pretty neat," George had admitted to JR when he, Nadya, and John returned from their outing to find all four dogs in bed and Kisa on the couch, having miraculously reappeared. "It even gave me some ideas for redecorating our apartment. Bones are pretty versatile, boy."

JR could only hope he was kidding.

"Keep reading, please," Masha told her father.

Niko continued: "The only confusing performance was that of the dog who wandered into the ring and began to howl. No one was quite sure whether it was an example of avant-garde performance art, or whether the dog was simply lost."

"Ooh." Robert flinched. "Sorry, bro. They totally didn't get it."

"That's all right," Pie said pensively. "Artists know not to take reviews to heart."

"Now show them the picture!" Masha cried, and Niko turned the newspaper around so everyone could see the photo that accompanied the article. In it, a fluffy grey cat balanced upside down on her tightrope, mesmerizing a crowd below.

"It's Kisa!" Nadya exclaimed.

"No way!" said George.

"Yes!" Masha scooped the cat up off the grass and gave her a hug. "Kisa helped save the show!"

"So that's where you went!" Nadya walked over and stroked Kisa's head. "You ran away to join the circus."

From over Masha's shoulder, Kisa gave JR a wink. "Something like that," she whispered.

"You must have had quite the adventure, Kisa," Nadya said, scratching her chin. "We're so glad you came home."

Masha looked up from the cat and gave her father a pointed look.

Niko cleared his throat again. "About that, Nadya," he said. "Kisa's act brought in a huge crowd. And it's been such a long time since we've had a tightrope act ..."

Nadya bit her lip and avoided her brother's gaze, as if she knew what was coming.

"We want to keep her in the circus, Tetya Nadya," Masha said softly. "Can we, please?"

Kisa looked from Nadya to Masha, then down to JR. "Really?" she said. "They want to keep me?"

"Of course," said JR. "You're one of the stars now."

"A star," Kisa whispered. "Wow. That's important."

"I was afraid you'd ask that." Nadya sighed. Then she smiled at her niece. "But how could I possibly say no? Kisa is so talented, and she obviously loves to perform."

Masha gave Kisa another squeeze, and the cat began to purr.

George put an arm around Nadya's shoulders. "That was really nice of you," he said.

Nadya smiled up at him. "It just makes sense. And anyway, we have a pet. A great one, at that."

JR's belly filled with warmth. He moved over to join his family.

"Hey, maybe when we get back to Moscow, we can adopt another cat," George suggested. "Would you like that?"

JR froze in mid-stride. *Another* cat? After all they'd been through?

"If you don't bite him, I will," Beatrix offered.

But Nadya shook her head. "No," she said, crouching to pet JR. He tilted his head so she could find the sweet spot behind his left ear. "I think I'm happy just the way things are."

Acknowledgments

Enormous thanks to all who helped me in the making of this novel, including but not limited to:

Jana Fernandes, for jogging my memory about the sights, sounds, and smells of Prague and letting me know when I was making things up.

The Inkslingers, who never fail to offer astute advice like, "You might want to show the circus."

Duncan Wall, who didn't know his reams of knowledge were contributing to a book about talking dogs, as I might have neglected to mention that.

Louise Delaney, who sat through some unsettling circus shows for the sake of my research. I'm sorry about the kangaroo. Also the woman suspended by her hair.

My agent, Marie Campbell, and the team at Puffin Canada, including Lynne Missen, Vikki VanSickle, Liza Morrison, and Catherine Dorton. Thanks a million.